Stranger on the River

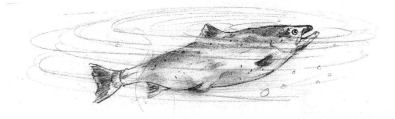

Stranger on the River

A novel of dastardly deeds on a Scottish salmon river

PAT GERBER

KAILYARDS PRESS

For Dorothy Carnie in her 100th year

First published in 1999 by Kailyards Press
6 Golf Road, Clarkston, Glasgow G76 7LZ

Cover painting and illustrations by Sue Gerber

Typeset by XL Publishing Services, Tiverton
Printed in Great Britain by The Cromwell Press, Trowbridge

Contents

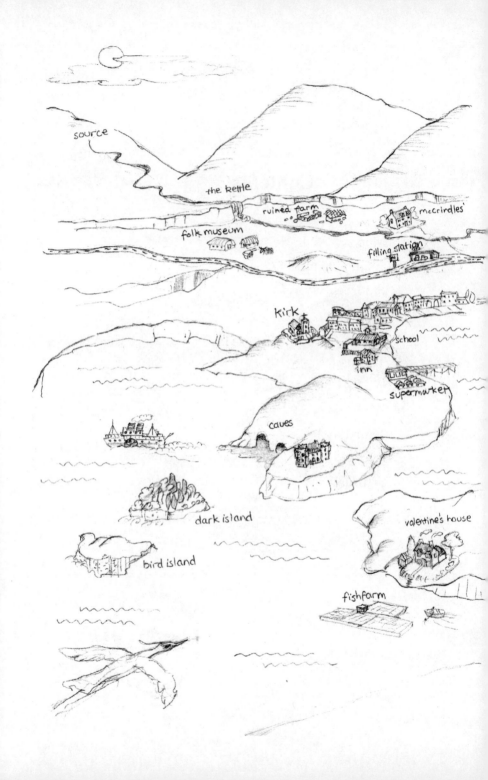

quarry

auld nick's

homefarm

salmon leap

stables

walled garden

munros

ardmellish house

farm

dunes

golf course

farm

hotel

N

W   E

S

Acknowledgements

Many people and organisations have given of their time and expertise to help me with this book. In particular I would like to thank the pupils of Primary 6, Braidbar Primary School, Giffnock, and their teachers Mrs Brass and Mrs Buchanan, also Jane Baker, Bryony Carnie, Colin Carnie, Indigo Carnie, Narinder Dhami, Cyril Gerber, Sue Hillman, Louise Jordan, Janice Lindsay, Alex McClelland, Robyn Marsack, David Paterson, Catriona Scott, Leslie Servant and Nancy Smith.

Saturday

Valentine relaxed against the beech tree's trunk, high among the new leaves. Whew, she was puffed out.

'PRIVATE, KEEP OUT. TRESPASSERS WILL BE PROSECUTED' warned the new notice at the entrance to Ardmellish Estate.

Climbing this tree, being in this place, was forbidden. She smiled to herself. If they wanted to prosecute her, they'd have to catch her first.

Far below her, the river Mellish poured over its waterfall, cascading into a deep black pool known as the Salmon Leap. She breathed in the damp smells of moss and distant sheep. She'd always loved this place. The Mellish was like a living thing, somewhere between an animal and a tree, with its own spirit. And right now, it needed her help.

Last winter the estate had been bought by a foreigner, nicknamed 'The Sheikh'. He'd stuck these disgusting acid-yellow PRIVATE notices at each entrance, villagers said, to keep poachers away. He'd padlocked every gate, coiled barbed wire over the stiles, sacked most of the workers, and swanned off to live in Spain, leaving Ardmellish House empty.

Valentine wanted to see if salmon truly jumped up waterfalls. How could a flabby fish leap such a height? She watched intently.

The birds had gone quiet and the sun was sliding behind the hills. A flittermouse flew by, its black batwings not much bigger than a butterfly. But nothing moved in the river. She'd better climb down and head home before it got dark.

What was that, crashing about in the bushes?

A bone-chilling howl echoed up. A large brown dog came lolloping along the path, nose to the ground. Oh no! It was Bounder the bloodhound. Bounder was even more terrifying than his bad-tempered owner, Auld Nick the gamekeeper, who kept him to scare people off. Right now, Valentine felt very scared indeed.

Bounder nosed about idly, lifted his leg, scuffed up a shower of earth and went to the edge of the pool to lap water noisily. He looked sloppy enough, his brown coat sagging about him as though it was several sizes too big, but she knew his wrinkly cheeks hid enormous teeth. There was no doubt she'd have to stay absolutely still until he went away. This was awkward. Mum would not be pleased if she was late home. And soon it would be dark.

Bounder lifted his head, sniffing the air. Then, very softly, he began to growl, the hair along his back rising. Valentine shivered, wishing she was safely home in the warm kitchen.

A heavily built man appeared beside the waterfall, his footfalls muffled by last winter's leaves. Bounder stood his ground, growling more fiercely.

'Get away, ye mangy cur,' snarled the man.

The big dog barked at him.

The man swung his boot, delivering a kick that sent Bounder yelping into the bushes.

Valentine was horrified. Although she was afraid of Bounder, the poor dog had only been doing his job.

The man seemed in no hurry. He lit a cigarette. Her tree shook slightly when he propped his back against it. Now she was looking straight down through the stubble that covered his bullet-shaped head to his greyish-white scalp.

Smoke swirled around. He inhaled deeply. She froze as his face turned upward, blowing out a stream of smoke. Could he see her? Apparently not. His expression didn't alter. Maybe the smoke, or the leaves, hid her? His face was fat and pale, like an overgrown baby's. His eyes were the most horrible she'd ever seen. They were scarlet, filled to the brim with blood.

To stop any more fear crawling up her veins, she concentrated on inventing a name for him. 'Bloodshot'.

With difficulty she forced herself to look away from Bloodshot's dreadful eyes, in case they focused on her. She hoped his cigarette fumes would not rise any higher, for smoke usually made her sneeze.

Bounder reappeared, prancing about like a puppy, making little yelps of joy and wagging his tail. Beside him walked a man he clearly thought of as a friend.

A scrub of reddish hair stuck out from under the grey fur hood of the man's parka. She'd call him – 'Fox-wolf'.

Fox-wolf carried a brush-handle, a length of fishing line and a metal contraption from which an assortment of huge barbed fish-hooks and lead weights gleamed in the dying light. From a short piece of rope dangled a dead salmon, head down. 'I got this wee fellow in the Bridge Pool,' he

called cheerfully. 'It'll feed ma family for a day or twa.'

Smoke rose from Bloodshot's mouth, 'Ye're late.' His voice was surprisingly high. 'Ain't ye supposed to be workin' the river for me tonight?' He threw the cigarette away.

'Sure, sir. I brought the jigger.' Fox-wolf lifted the contraption. 'Hey Bounder, man, I hope ye havenae brought yer maister.' He bent to stroke the dog's head. 'Oh, ye've been in the wars – is that blood on yer belly?'

Bloodshot spat. 'Leave the stupid animal alone. Ye've work to do.' He pulled out his mobile phone, yanked up the aerial, pushed some buttons then hissed 'Fanshawe – can you 'ear me, Fanshawe?'

Fox-wolf waved his arm at Bounder. 'Awa hame tae yer maister.'

The big dog looked at him, then trotted off into the bushes.

Up on her branch, Valentine understood. These men were poachers. They were here to steal fish from the river. An idea popped into her head. Pulling a small tape-recorder out of her pocket, slipping the cord round her wrist so it couldn't fall, she pressed the 'record' button.

Bloodshot was cursing into his mobile, turning around, bending from side to side as if doing exercises; 'Ye're breaking up – I can't 'ear yer Fanshawe . . . Okay – ye're down at the bridge keepin' an eye out for the cops. Well, don't fall asleep this time, right?'

Oh no! A huge sneeze was trying to happen in her head. Valentine grabbed her nose and pinched hard. She almost fell out of the tree. The stopped sneeze felt like it would blow the back of her brains out, but it made no sound.

Fox-wolf laid his salmon under a bush. He began to sort out his poaching gear, talking softly over his shoulder to Bloodshot. 'They say the bailiff's away to a ceilidh in Lochgilphead. He'll be dancin' till dawn, so I'm thinkin' we'll no' be troubled wi' him tonight.'

Bloodshot snorted snot up his nose. 'I've a score to settle with that Gavin McCrindle. He may be the bailiff here now – but it was 'im as got me put away five year ago, when 'e were a copper.'

'Och, man, a bailiff's nothin' but a policeman in fancy clothes, set on tae stop the poachin.'

Bloodshot spat again. 'Once a copper always a copper. But I'll get even with 'im, you'll see.'

The two men sloshed into the river. Valentine switched off the recorder. At last. The chance to escape. The sound of the waterfall would drown any noise she might make.

She started the climb down, negotiating her way as carefully as she could from one bough to the next, keeping an eye on the poachers. She hung from the last branch, ready to drop to the ground and run, when from just below her feet came a low growl.

Bounder!

Somehow, she wriggled up till she was out of his reach. He stood up, his paws almost on the branch, sniffing and whining.

'Go home, Bounder,' she whispered, climbing up to where she'd been, as fast as she could.

Bounder slouched away into the shadows.

She thought about what to do. Obviously she was stuck, till the poachers – and Bounder – had gone. But, meantime, she could watch. If she got out of this in one piece, she'd at least be able to describe them. She must remember every detail of what they did.

Filled with horror, she looked on, as the moon rose, dappling the black water with silver.

Again and again Bloodshot and Fox-wolf raked the river with the cruel jigger, foul-hooking the fish in their backs, their sides, their bellies, flinging the gleaming, writhing bodies onto the rocks. Soon a dozen salmon lay there, flapping in their death agonies, no longer shining but dark with blood.

What could an eleven-year-old girl do to stop the carnage? If Valentine dared to confront the men, at best they'd laugh at her, and at worst – well, you were always being warned not to go near strangers.

What if they went on poaching all night? Perhaps Mum would be phoning the police right now. Hey, if this was a story in a book, the police would come looking for *her*, and find the poachers! Everyone would be so thankful to catch the criminals they'd forget to be cross with her. The only problem was, she hadn't actually mentioned to Mum that she was coming here. Because no way would Mum have said yes to trespassing.

She squirmed as she thought what her punishment might be. She'd definitely be grounded. Yet it was vital that this week, of all weeks, she wasn't kept in.

She shivered, feeling cold and stiff. If only she could go home.

How come she'd got herself into this mess? It was because of a dog.

Yesterday, the teacher brought her black and white collie dog Lia to the school in a terrible state, two of its paws swathed in bandages. 'I want you to see this,' Mrs McCrindle, clearly upset, lifted Lia on to a table.

'What happened to her, Miss?' wee Sadie piped up, reaching out to stroke Lia's rough coat.

'Careful, Sadie. Lia may be a little nervous today.' Mrs

McCrindle took a piece of bandage and made a neat muzzle by tying it around the dog's mouth and behind its ears. 'Lia's paws have been cut to ribbons by broken glass. Why do picnickers have to smash their bottles? Lia must have been tempted by their left-over sandwiches.'

Lia stood with her head hanging down, looking hopefully at the children. Perhaps someone would feel sorry for her and give her a titbit?

Valentine couldn't help laughing at the dog's expression, while feeling really sorry for her. 'Why don't we start a club,' she said, 'to clean up the seashore and the riverbanks?'

They dreamed up a name for it – 'Friends of the River Mellish', FORM. They'd have a newsletter. She'd interview Ardmellish residents for their opinions about the local environment and write them up. So Mrs McCrindle had lent her the school's little tape-recorder. Today she'd recorded lots of comments and suggestions from people. And this evening she'd ducked under the PRIVATE notice to make a start clearing rubbish up here around the Salmon Leap. The bag was now full of bottles, cans and tangles of fishing line.

A howl from deep in the wood jerked Valentine's thoughts back to the present.

Bounder was baying again. Peering through the gloom, she saw Bloodshot and Fox-wolf come splashing out of the river. On the bank, they kicked the dying salmon into a heap, then stuffed them into sacks.

Oh good, they'd be going now.

But no, here they were, coming under her tree again. The

click of her tape-recorder ON button sounded horribly loud.

Bloodshot lit another cigarette. His words drifted up with the coils of smoke. 'I've an order that'll make your day, mate.'

Fox-wolf wiped his hands on his trousers and the silver fish-scales gleamed in the moonlight. 'Oh aye? I could be doin' wi' something.'

At that moment, Bloodshot's mobile began bleeping. He pulled it out. 'Ello. Fanshawe? The police patrol's gawn? Good. We've got us a li'l load 'ere. Meet us at the bridge with the van, right?' His laugh turned into a coughing fit.

Fox-wolf began tying up the sacks.

Bloodshot pocketed his mobile. 'We've some planning to do, mate. A big refrigerated van to fill, Friday night – '

'Man, where are you goin' to get one o' them?'

'No problema, mate. I'm in the business, you might say. So I 'ope you're not plannin' on takin' yer missus out nor nothingk.'

'How will you an' me fill a whole van? Ye'll never dae it wi' jiggerin.'

'Na, jiggering's no good. We 'ardly caught nothink tonight.'

'Nettin' then? Is it dynamite you're talkin'? A wee underwater explosion tae stun the fish afore we net them?'

'And 'ave all the cops from miles around 'earing the bang and catchin' us red-'anded? Not likely. Wotever else, mate, it'll 'ave to be quiet. I'm not doin' time again for no-one. No way.'

Fox-wolf shook his head. 'I'm no usin' poison, if that's your idea.'

'There ain't no point using anythink else, mate.'

'What – suffocate every livin' thing from here down to the sea-loch? There'd be nae fishin' in the river Mellish for years, afterwards. No. I cannae stomach that. Not on this river, that I've ghillied on since I wis a boy. Man, I've spent ma life lookin' after it, and my faither and grandfaither afore me.'

'Yer father and yer grandfather ain't 'ere to 'elp you now. Listen, mate, if we do the job proper, there'll be enough money in it to send you and me off to Spain for a wile. Think of it – the wife and kiddies with a pool of their own to swim in, and all the sun they can take. And when the 'eat's died down 'ere, you can come 'ome. If you want to. Wot more could a man ask?' Bloodshot pulled out a bundle of money. 'See that? That's only a fraction of wot you'll 'ave. D'you want it, or not?'

Fox-wolf swallowed noisily, gawping at the money. His hood fell back.

Shocked, Valentine realised who he was. Coll Munro's dad.

Bloodshot's tone roughened. 'My contact needs every fish from this river as weighs over two pound. Take it – or leave it.'

'I'll no' dae it. And that's my last word.'

Bloodshot blew a long stream of smoke up into the tree. 'Not even to get back at the Sheikh?'

Fox-wolf groaned, putting his head in his hands for a moment. 'The Sheikh? Aye, tae teach him a lesson, maybe. I'm that scunnered wi' him. He's no' feart to charge fancy prices to the business-men for their fishin', but he laid all of us off, to save himself payin' our wages. Efficiency, he called it.'

Smoke surrounded Bloodshot's head. His voice was silky-smooth. ''undreds of thousands of pounds . . .'

'And he'd stand to lose the toffs' ticket fees, for there'd be nae fish left for them . . .'

'Nah yer talkin'. Can you get 'old of the stuff?'

'The poison? Auld Nick'll hae a tin or two.'

'Mister Nicholas the game-keeper wot 'as that mangy

'ound? 'Ow'll you get it orf 'im?'

Valentine's nose was tickling badly. She buried it in her sleeve, pressing the sneeze in while she kept her recorder on, collecting the poachers' plans till the tape clicked off, finished.

Bloodshot threw the burning stub of his cigarette into the pool. It hissed briefly. He picked up the blood-streaked sacks of dead fish. 'This lot's for the 'otel. Back door. Dosh for the weekend. No questions asked.' He laughed unpleasantly. 'Right then. Friday it is. The old bridge. At sunset. Be there. And mate, don't forget the poison.'

'Trust me.' Davy Munro pulled up the hood of his parka. He began threading his fish through the hem, so that only its tail hung out. 'Makes yer jaicket hing better,' he grinned.

Bloodshot moved away. 'Give me five minutes start – in case there's anyone about. I didn't like the sound of that dog.' Dragging the sacks, he waddled away, out of sight.

Splash! A salmon sprang at the waterfall, its silver skin lit by a moonbeam. It leaped again, and again, but the river was too powerful, and the fish fell back into the dark pool.

Davy Munro dug in his pocket. Producing the stub-end of a cigarette, he stuck it in his mouth. He scraped a match against the bark, cupping the flame with his hand, inhaling. A stream of smoke filtered up through the branches. Heaving a sigh, he headed out into the moonlight.

Valentine's nose began to tingle even more. For as long as she could, she held the sneeze in, but suddenly it came, blasting out of her nostrils, and echoing through the trees.

Davy Munro stopped stock still. 'Who's that?'

The silent wood waited.

Just as her second sneeze came, Bounder's bark echoed again through the wood. He came loping down the path. She saw his dark shape speeding under the tree, nose to the ground, following Bloodshot's scent? Behind him trotted a small bandy-legged figure, cursing angrily 'Bounder, come in to heel. It's only rabbits, you useless dog.'

Davy Munro stepped forward, his hand over the salmon's tail. 'Evenin' Mr Nicholas, sir.'

'Davy?'

'Aye. I was just takin' a wee stroll. That's a grand dog you've got there. Are you headin' my way?'

❧ • ❧

Not till a good half-hour after the two men had disappeared, Bounder safely secured on a lead, did Valentine dare to climb down from her perch. The moon helped her see.

She had never felt so scared in her life. Every shadow seemed to have the huge shape of Bloodshot. The dark wood was full of strange noises, hootings and scrabblings.

Shaking with fear and tiredness, she followed the path. It looked so different from in daytime. An unearthly screech echoed. She nearly jumped out of her skin, then recognised the sound. It was a fox barking.

At last she reached the main road. The orange street-lights from the village had never looked more welcoming. She ran along the beach towards the point at the far end where her house perched. One upstairs window had a light on. She rubbed her nose, which was still tickly from the poachers' cigarette smoke.

Carefully she tried the back door. It opened with a small creak. Hoping Mum would be asleep, she crept into the dark kitchen. And then she really sneezed.

Sunday

The kitchen light snapped on. Mrs Kerr stood there, frowning. 'Valentine, where on earth have you been? It's after midnight.'

Tears prickled the back of Valentine's eyes. She was exhausted, and starving. 'Sorry, Mum.' She looked at the bowl of fruit on the table.

Mrs Kerr sat her down on a chair. 'I want the full story, right now. Are you okay?'

'It wasn't my fault, Mum.' Unable to wait another minute for food, Valentine took an apple and bit into its sour flesh. 'There were these poachers at the Salmon Leap and I – '

'The Salmon Leap? But Valentine, the estate's out of bounds!'

'Yes but – ' she couldn't get the words out straight. 'I got stuck up the beech tree – '

'Got stuck up a tree? Valentine, I was going frantic. Phoning everyone I could think of.'

Valentine stared at the apple. Its white flesh was turning brown at the edges. 'I didn't know what to do. So I waited till they – till he'd gone.' She was feeling wretchedly guilty. Her mum sounded so cross, yet there were tears in her eyes.

Mrs Kerr blew her nose loudly. 'I was worried sick. Everyone must have been at the ceilidh – nothing but answering machines. Even at the bailiff's and the police station. Not much good if there was an emergency in the village.' She sat bolt upright, 'Poacher? What poacher?'

Valentine hung her head so that her hair fell down over her face. For some reason she couldn't tell the full story. She only told about Coll Munro's dad.

'Oh Val. Davy Munro's a harmless-enough fellow.' Mrs Kerr put her arms round Valentine. 'Everyone knows he does a bit of poaching. He wouldn't have harmed you. Thank goodness you're all right. Now, some hot chocolate and a toastie and up to bed with you. You look tired out.'

❦ • ❦

In the kitchen next morning, Valentine yawned. Her mother was up to the elbows in flour. 'Come on, we've a baking to do.' Mrs Kerr tied the strings of her apron more firmly.

Valentine unwisely pulled a face. 'Oh no. Not baking. Not today.' She longed to escape. The sun was shining, and everyone would be down on the beach by now.

But her mother was rattling bowls and tins out of the cupboard. 'Flour, sugar and butter please, Val. We'll do a big batch of scones first, then a couple of cakes.'

'You can buy really nice scones and cakes in the shop.'

'No chance. I like to know what's in my food.'

'But mum – '

'Look, Valentine, tomorrow I have to deal with a delivery of smolts. It's a holiday Monday, we'll have no workers, and your father won't be back from his Organic Fish Farming conference till the end of the week. I can't believe it's almost six months since we bought this place.'

23

'Okay.' Valentine knew when she was beaten. 'But then can I go?'

'We'll see. I've got to do enough to fill the freezer, for all the days when I don't have time to cook. Now – flour – '

Valentine switched on Radio 1 full blast and heaved a sigh of resignation.

'And baking-powder. That red tin. Oh, it's nearly finished.' Mrs Kerr plonked the scales on the table, heaving an equally long sigh. 'I'd rather have Radio 3 or 4. Now, let's hear about Davy Munro and his poaching. What exactly did you see?'

While they worked, Valentine told a bit more about what she'd seen the previous night. But she kept quiet about Bloodshot and his plan for Friday. If Mum discovered a dangerous gang was operating in the area, she'd never be let out to play again. It would be like when they lived in the town, having to be driven everywhere, having no freedom.

Mrs Kerr rolled out the scone dough. 'You cut out, Val, while I make a start on the cakes.'

Valentine began stamping out scones. The kitchen smelt warm and floury. Raisins kept sticking to the cutter. She looked disgustedly at her efforts. 'They're as thin as biscuits.'

Mrs Kerr sprinkled a little flour on the oven trays. 'Only because they haven't risen yet. The chemicals in the baking powder – you know, a mix of acid and alkali – they fizz up when you add liquid. In the oven the heat makes the bubbles bigger, so the scones rise. The cooking sets them. See?'

'Right.' Valentine's mind wasn't totally concentrating.

'How are things at school, Val?'

'Okay.'

'Mrs McCrindle says she's pleased with your work, but you're a bit of a day-dreamer. You must be getting to know a few of the kids by now.'

'Hmph. They call us "the White Settlers".'

'It can't be that bad. What about the McCrindle kid? He was always friendly enough when we came on holiday.'

'Alan's okay. But he won't come out much. He's a computer nut. There's Coll Munro but – '

'But?'

Valentine tried to stop sugar and butter flying everywhere as the paddle of the ancient mixer whirled round.

'Coll seems a nice lad.' Mrs Kerr switched off the mixer. 'He's maybe a bit – slow.'

Valentine stuck her finger in the cake-mixture and licked it thoughtfully. 'I used to think Coll was great.'

'Used to?'

'Coll knows everything – about the river. But – if his dad's a poacher – oh, I don't know.'

'Careful, Val.' Mrs Kerr gave the mixture a last stir. 'It's easy to start rumours, difficult to stop them. Gossip can harm perfectly innocent people.'

'How do you mean?'

'Think about it. You could ruin Davy's chances of a job with this story.' Mrs Kerr scraped mixture into a cake tin. 'Apparently he was a very good ghillie, once upon a time. Mr Nicholas – '

'Auld Nick?'

'Mr Nicholas has been the gamekeeper since the old family lived at Ardmellish House. But now he's turned sour and people don't understand. I think it's overwork. He was very upset when Mr Hassan sacked Davy.'

'The Sheikh?'

25

Mrs Kerr nodded. 'Davy came from a long line of ghillies, who looked after the rivers while the gamies kept the woods and the hills. And I think Mr Nicholas will be doing everything he can to get Davy reinstated.'

'Coll wants to be a ghillie when he grows up. Mum, how can I tell –?'

'Tell?'

'If Coll knows – about his dad poaching?'

Mrs Kerr slid trayfuls of scones into the oven. 'Don't be so dramatic. You'd hardly class what Davy does as a major crime, dear.'

The kitchen, and the two of them, soon acquired a fine dusting of flour, and as one batch after another went into the oven, the room filled with wonderful smells. Eventually Valentine was given a hot buttered scone in her hand, and her freedom for the afternoon.

'Mum, can I borrow Dad's trout rod?'

The phone rang. It was one of Mum's friends and she launched herself into a saga about the difficulties of organic fish-farming. Valentine grabbed the rod and fled.

❦

Running along the beach towards the village, the wind blowing against her, Valentine's brain whirled in circles. Somehow she must find a way to stop Bloodshot poisoning the river. But no way could she tell Mum about him. Should she go and see Stuart the policeman? Or Mr McCrindle the bailiff? But then, they might tell Mum.

A cloud came over the sun.

At the village end of the beach, a knot of people gathered around the teacher Mrs McCrindle. She was Alan's mum, and everybody liked her. She was holding forth. 'Children,

as you know, my husband Gavin is the water bailiff in this area. It's his job to look after all the rivers and the seashore. He's been finding all sorts of dangerous rubbish lying about – fishing line, nets, poly bags – all a terrible danger to animals, birds and fish. We must persuade visitors to take their litter home!'

Sometimes Mrs McCrindle could sound quite heroic. Valentine almost clapped.

'Hello, Valentine,' the teacher called. 'Come and join us. How did you get on yesterday?'

Puffing after her run, Valentine described her recording session by the pier. Some people wouldn't speak, like Coll and Sadie's mum, who could only giggle shyly, and others only wanted to complain about things like the price of milk these days, or the shortage of buses, but she'd managed to fill both sides of one tape, and start a new one, before she was done.

'Well done, Valentine,' said the teacher. 'And you're going to try writing out some of the comments, for the FORM newsletter?'

'Yes, Miss.'

Alan had agreed to print the newsletter. Coll had said he'd help when he could, but had to bring wee Sadie because their mum was doing a cleaning job up at the big house, since their dad had been made redundant. And Mrs McCrindle had offered to spend a few of her own Sunday afternoons to give fishing lessons 'As a reward for your hard work' to any interested member of FORM.

Valentine looked around the group. Six of the boys were waving fishing rods around. None of the girls had turned up except wee Sadie, and she didn't count.

Mrs McCrindle stood out in front of them demonstrating. 'The shore's a good place to learn,' she trilled. 'Plenty of space, so you won't get your lines stuck in the trees, or in each other's hair.'

The boys lined up with an assortment of rods borrowed from their grandfathers or big brothers. Valentine joined at the far end, between Alan and Coll. She couldn't meet Coll's eyes. She took the rod out of its cover and managed to fix it together, but she had difficulty with the reel.

'Gie it tae me.' Coll attached the reel effortlessly to the cork handle.

'Let me do it myself,' said Valentine, grabbing it back. She threaded the line along through the holding rings. Tying on the cast was tricky. The short length of fine nylon thread seemed to have a mind of its own, wriggling about and coming loose the minute she let go.

'Watch me, children. Casting is a simple movement, like this – ' Mrs McCrindle drew the rod back over her shoulder, 'and this – ' she swept it forward so that the fishing line flew ahead of her in a smooth curve, landing almost straight down the beach. 'The idea is to cast your fly exactly to the spot on the river where you think the fish might be lying. It takes – a little practice.'

'Can you help me, Miss?' asked Valentine.

Mrs McCrindle showed her how to tie her cast on correctly. 'We're just using small weights today' she said, selecting one from Valentine's box. 'No hooks, till you can cast well enough not to catch anything you don't want. Coll, you go first. Aim at that clump of seaweed. Watch him everyone – Coll's a natural.'

Turning scarlet, Coll cast an almost perfect line, which landed on the seaweed.

Mrs McCrindle looked pleased. 'Right children. Have a go.'

It looked easy, like cracking a whip in slow motion. But

try as she would, Valentine could not make her line fly out.

Neither could Alan. Time and again his line ended up in knots around the top of his rod as he lashed the air. He was pink with embarrassment.

Valentine felt sorry for him. 'Coll's a natural,' she mimicked in his mother's voice.

Alan smiled gratefully and tried again.

While they practised, Mrs McCrindle was in full voice. 'You are the Friends of the River Mellish. We catch two kinds of fish in the Mellish, do you know what they are?'

Wee Sadie squeaked 'Me and my daddy's caught sticklebacks and minnows in my jeely jar. And sometimes in our pond there's tadpoles that turns into frogs.'

Coll snarled, 'Aw shut up, Sadie.'

But Mrs McCrindle said, 'Sticklebacks and minnows. Good, Sadie. But what about bigger fish, ones we can eat? Coll?'

'Like trout, Miss, and salmon?'

'That's right, Coll. Trout, which live in the river all the year round, and salmon, which don't.'

Back and forward went her rod as she spoke. 'Let's talk about salmon. The more you learn about salmon the more you realise what wonderful creatures they are. Do you know, when they are smolts, only a few inches long, they swim all the way from the rivers of Scotland across the Atlantic Ocean to Greenland? There, they feast on krill, tiny pink shrimpy things. They grow fat and their flesh turns pink, and they mature into grilse. We don't know what makes them then decide to come home to Scotland, or Ireland, or Norway – '

Coll piped up, 'It's the Irn-Bru, Miss.'

'Thank you, Coll. Whatever it is, instinct perhaps, the mature salmon swim back across the Atlantic to form great

shoals off the Western Isles. They then split up and return to the rivers from which they came. Throughout the spring and summer, they fight their way upriver, often having to leap waterfalls and rapids, till they reach shallow gravel beds. There they lay their eggs and the whole cycle begins again. After spawning they're exhausted and thin, for they never eat in fresh water – '

'Just as well,' said Alan, laying down his rod, 'what with all the rubbish we found yesterday.'

'They slip away downriver, as kelts, coloured brown by the peaty water of the river. If someone accidentally catches a kelt they must put it back, so that it has the chance to return to the Atlantic feeding grounds.' She picked up Alan's rod and put it back in his hand. 'I know you're happier on the computer, son, but keep trying. And you too, Valentine. Coll, that's excellent. Your father's taught you well.'

Coll blushed again. 'It was my grandad. My Daddy says I'm no' tae waste my time wi' the river, the way he did. I've tae go to the university and be a lawyer or the like. No' like him, finished by the time he's forty.' Then he grinned sheepishly, his blush fading. 'Mind you, I've no' got the brains tae be a lawyer. So maybe I'll get tae stay here after all.'

Mrs McCrindle smiled. All the time Coll was speaking, Valentine watched him for signs of guilt. But he just looked his normal dozy self. She began to feel better about him.

Mrs McCrindle untangled her line for the hundredth time. 'Try to follow Coll's rhythm, see?' She drew Valentine's arm back, paused for a second, then pushed it forward easily. It worked better. Valentine caught Coll grinning at her. She gritted her teeth and kept going, while the teacher went to the far end of the row to help the younger children.

As she worked the rod back and forth, Valentine heard some of the other boys sniggering behind her back, 'Girls canny fish. Specially no' white settler girls.'

Coll, by now, was showing off, tossing his rod above his head in great style, flicking his line forward easily. 'It's men that catches salmon.'

He always had to be one of the gang, thought Valentine, telling everyone how brilliant he was. She reckoned he was trying to get her mad, so she pretended not to hear.

All his pals were giggling and making stupid faces at her.

Valentine lashed out her line more firmly.

Mrs McCrindle called, 'That's much better, Valentine. And what were you saying, Coll?'

'Nothin', Miss.'

'You might be interested to know that the biggest salmon ever was hooked by a Scots lassie.' Mrs McCrindle walked along the row. 'Georgina Ballantine, she was called. Sixty-four pounds, it weighed! It took her two and a half hours to land, and was the same length as herself. The second biggest was caught on the Deveron by a Miss Morisson – sixty-three pounds. Women often have the knack. I can get a fish when Gavin can't – even though he's the bailiff!'

'Dad's better at catching poachers' said Alan.

Valentine sent her line curling back. She let it hang for a second, then brought the rod forward to send it singing out silkily to run its full length, straight along the beach, at last.

'Brilliant,' said the teacher. 'Perhaps we'll try you out on the river one day.'

Valentine saw Coll making a face at Alan, who grinned back. She felt mad at him, and perplexed. She wanted to discuss the poaching plot with the boys, but how could she when they were being so infantile?

'Time to pack up.' Mrs McCrindle helped the younger children.

Valentine ran after the boys as they walked up the beach. The words were out before she could stop them, 'Anyway, Coll Munro, your dad's a dirty poacher.'

'What?' Alan was still laughing.

'I saw his father last night. At the Salmon Leap. He was with a horrible guy. A poacher. They were killing the fish. And they're going to poison our river and steal all the salmon. On Friday night.'

Coll's eyebrows shot up. 'Eh? That's no' true.'

'I heard them. And I taped them. On this.' She produced the recorder from her pocket. 'I can prove it.'

Coll frowned, 'C'mon Sadie. We're no' listenin' tae a white settler lassie that tells lies. Our Daddy wid never dae a thing like that.' He pulled at Sadie's hand.

'What's a poachah?' Sadie hung back.

'Aw shut up, Sadie.' Coll dragged her across the road.

Valentine yelled after him 'Your Dad's a poacher, Coll Munro. And – and so are you.' She was smarting from the boys' laughter and couldn't help quite enjoying the fact that she'd made him angry.

Coll was running away up the track to their house, Sadie trailing after him.

Alan said, 'What are you on about, Val?'

She said, 'It's true. Listen to this.' With a triumphant flourish, she switched on the tape-recorder. A low growling sound faded into silence.

'Oh no, what's up with it? wailed Valentine.

Alan stood waiting. 'Batteries done?'

Valentine, deeply disappointed, nodded. 'I must have forgotten to switch if off last night. And the shop won't be open till Tuesday.'

'You'd better tell me all about it, anyway.'

When Valentine had finished, he was thoughtful. 'There's always a bit of poaching around this time of year, because it's when the salmon start coming up the river to the spawning beds. That's why Dad gets a summer bailiff in to help him. I've heard him talk about other rivers being poisoned, right enough, but never the Mellish.' He looked thoughtful. 'Give me the recorder. I'll find batteries for it and play it to Dad tonight.'

'No!' She stuffed it back into her pocket.

'Why not? It's his job to stop poaching.'

'Because – because he'd tell my Mum. Definitely. If she gets to hear about this, she'll never let me out again. We've got to deal with this ourselves.'

'Don't be crazy, Val.'

'I'm serious.' She was near to tears.

Alan fixed her with a stare. 'And what's more important – the river, or your problem mother?'

Valentine looked down. 'I'll – think of something. At least don't tell him till – till tomorrow night. If I haven't had an idea what to do by then,' she shrugged, 'then I suppose you'll have to.'

'Okay. But no longer. If it's true, then it's too important. Oh,' He brightened. 'We could put it in the FORM newsletter. Did you write it?'

Valentine produced a sheet of crumpled and soggy paper. 'Don't know if you'll be able to read it. I didn't have much time.'

'Friends of the River Mellish Newsletter no. 1,' he read. 'Yep. It looks okay. I'll put it on Dad's computer tonight. See you.' And he went off in the direction of his home.

A burst of rain swept across the loch, blotting out the horizon.

Valentine wandered round the curving beach, heading towards the fish farm on the point, the wet wind buffeting her this way and that.

Five days, she thought. Five days till Friday. And by tomorrow she had to come up with an idea to stop the poisoning, or Alan would tell his father, and the news would be all round the village, and her mother would keep her in, just like she used to in the town.

Monday

Coll woke up feeling uncomfortable. For a start, something heavy was lying across his stomach. He opened his eyes. His dog, Bracken, gazed at him, her deep brown eyes hopeful of interesting walks, preferably with rabbit chases and titbits.

'Get off, Bracken.' He tried to heave her over. It wasn't so easy. She was a big dog, half greyhound, half doberman, the colour of a ripe chestnut, and she was stubborn.

She stuck her wet nose into his face and licked him sloppily.

'Ugh.' He stroked her silky ear. She was gentle-natured and affectionate at home and with their friends, only fierce with people she didn't know. Over the top of her head, he watched the rain drops trickling down his tiny attic window-pane and wished he could get his brain to work more quickly.

What was nagging away at the back of his mind? If he

thought for a while, perhaps it would come clearer, like mud settling in a puddle.

Outside, his father's voice sang 'Viva España' with great expression.

That was it. Valentine Kerr said his dad was going to poison the salmon in the river. She'd said, 'He was with a horrible guy.' Who could it have been? What was going on?

'Coll?' Sadie stood in the doorway in her droopy green dress. She held out a bent-looking sandwich. Her large blue eyes wore an expression which was meant to be appealing. 'Mammy says you're tae get up. I made a piece and jam for ye.'

'What is it ye want, Sadie?' he bit hungrily into the bread. He knew when she was trying to bribe him.

'Nothin',' Sadie said, her face crumpling.

'Aw Sadie – I didnae mean – ' But she'd gone. Now he felt like a bully. Sadie wasn't really too bad, for a wee sister. But – no-one else had a wee sister trailing after them all the time.

He gave the last corner of the sandwich to Bracken, who sniffed it with her black nose, looked up at him to make sure it was meant for her, and took it delicately.

He shoved her off the bed and got dressed slowly, enjoying the thought that it was a holiday Monday, and there would be no school.

His mother's voice floated up the attic stair, 'Get a move on Coll. I'm awa' tae ma work. Ye'll need tae watch wee Sadie for us, the day.'

The kitchen smelled of boiling fish. Munching another piece and jam, he wandered outside. Beneath the trees, bluebells drooped. Tiny fern fronds unfurled among them like green question-marks and the air smelt of wet flowers. Bracken splashed in and out of the wood, nose to the ground, imagining rabbits round every tree-trunk. The nearby river sounded as if it was in spate, full after the rain. How he loved his home. He couldn't imagine ever wanting to live anywhere else.

His father was in the open-sided woodshed, tinkering with the engine of his old Yamaha bike. 'Is that you off wi' yer mates then, son?'

Coll shrugged. He stood watching his father in silence for a moment, munching his crust. He loved his father too, but what if he wasn't a good man? What then? Valentine might be telling everyone his dad was a 'dirty poacher.' How could he face his friends? Yet somehow, he must.

His Dad revved the Yamaha's engine. It sputtered, then backfired loudly.

A Landrover rumbled into view along the bumpy track. The bailiff slid open the window. 'I thought someone was taking a pot-shot at me, Davy. Is it not time you were throwing that old bike on the tip?'

'Gavin McCrindle, man, it's yersel'. Och she's just needin' a wee bit oil. She'll dae me fine – till I win the lottery.'

The big man got out. 'I'll not keep you long, Davy. Just a wee word?'

'Och, I'm no' goin' anywhere, these days. Come awa' in. I was just thinkin' o' a cup o' tea. Coll, you'll be puttin' the kettle on for the bailiff.'

Sadie appeared up the track, gathering bluebells, Bracken prancing around her. Coll felt jealous, as if Bracken might sometimes like Sadie better than him.

Turning his back on them, he went indoors, followed by the two men. The smell of cooked salmon hung in the air. He got out three mugs, teabags, sugar and milk. He liked listening to the men talking. If you kept quiet and didn't bother them, you could learn things.

His dad poured strong black tea into the mugs. 'And how was yon ceilidh?'

'Och, wild,' said the bailiff. 'Lachy the post had his accordion. These Lochgilphead folk know how to dance!'

'You'll have a wee bit of a sore head maybe, Gavin, man?'

'You're not wrong there.' The bailiff clutched his temples exaggeratedly.

Coll stirred spoonfuls of sugar into his tea to make it less bitter. The men talked generally for a while, about the weather, the rainy Spring, the latest antics of the fishing syndicate. Then the bailiff got up, casually. 'That'll be a wee bit fish you're cooking?' He lifted the lid off the fish-kettle.

Coll almost choked. Somehow Dad had acquired a salmon last night. Had he bought it – or stolen it? His mind began to clear. This would be a good test – would his father tell the truth?

Davy looked out of the window. 'Aye. A bonny wee grilse. A friend was passing – you know?'

Coll glanced at the bailiff.

Gavin wandered over to look out of the window. 'Aye, aye.'

'Och, Gavin man. A fish is a wild thing. It doesn't come intae the world wi' a landowner's name on it. Will you take a wee dram, now?'

The bailiff shook his head. 'Not while I'm working. You're a terrible fellow, Davy Munro.' He turned to face him. 'But you'll need to take care. There's a few nasty folk about, this weather. Young Stuart the police was just saying so, last night.'

Coll watched a dark flush rise over his father's face.

'Is that a fact?' Dad was angry now. 'Well, maybe the Sheikh shouldnae have got rid of so many of us, last year. There was always plenty of estate workers and that about the river, when the old family had the place, to keep nasty folks away. That's what a ghillie like myself was for.'

'I know, Davy, and I'm sorry. But things change. Did you read in the paper about the ghillie that was shot last week, in Central?'

'We cannae afford a newspaper now.'

'Poachers, it was. And they're not caught yet. Stuart reckons it'll be a big gang from the town. There's a lot of rivers been troubled by them in Central Scotland. We know they're a big organised gang, walkie-talkies, refrigerated vans, night sights, guns, the lot. And this year they're using – poison in the rivers. They'll have the fish back in Glasgow by morning, and away to the markets in the south. Now the police in Central have got their number, it looks like they're moving further west. And they're not afraid to shoot anyone that gets in their way.'

'Well, man, if I was the ghillie – '

'Och, Davy, if I had any say in the matter, you still would be. And it's a good help to me that you're still taking an interest in the river. I know you'd tell me if you saw anything unusual, – any strangers about, like.'

Coll saw his father's head go down. Why wouldn't he look at Mr McCrindle, man to man?

The bailiff got up to go. 'I'm pleased enough that the Fisheries Board has at last seen fit to give me money to pay a temporary bailiff, to help out over the summer, when the poaching's at its worst.'

'Aye, auld Fanshawe's daughter.'

'Don't sound so sour, Davy. She maybe comes over a bit posh, but she's been fishing the river with her dad since she was a wee lassie. He asked me to take her on – she'd been in a wee bit of bother, and he thought some work in the country would maybe sort her out.'

'So it's easier tae get a job if you've been in bother.'

The big man clapped Coll's father on the shoulder. 'Davy, you're worth a lot more than the kind of pay a seasonal gets, and you'd have lost all your benefits. Something will turn up.'

'Aye maybe.'

'I've a meeting tomorrow – to introduce her to Auld Nick.' The big man laughed. 'We don't want him taking pot shots at Miss Fanshawe by mistake. In the mean time, Davy, you keep an eye on the river – and I'll not be noticing what you're cooking.' He eyed the fish-kettle, winked at Coll, and strode out of the house.

Bracken trotted in through the open door. She stopped, one paw in the air, her eye on Coll. She wanted him to take her for a walk.

'I'm away out,' Coll said.

'Aye, right. That's the rain off now. And ye'll be takin' wee Sadie wi' you, son?'

'Och, Daddy. Me and my pals – we're no' wantin' a wean.'

Sadie, who always seemed to know what was going on, appeared at her father's knee. 'I'll be no bother,' she wheedled.

His father gave her a hug, 'My wee Sadie's never any bother,' he cooed.

Sadie smirked, rubbing her face on her father's jacket, and turning her blue eyes on Coll.

Coll was furious. 'Aw Daddy.' But he knew when he was beaten. He gave his father a sour look. Weren't men supposed to stick together?

'Keep an eye on her, man,' said his father.

'C'mon, Sadie.' Coll sounded crosser than he really felt, stomping out of the house. Bracken ran to and fro across the track. He wanted to be proud of his dad, but he had just this minute heard him tell a lie to the bailiff, who was supposed to be his friend.

He needed time to think. Was it possible that his father was up to no good? Somehow, he'd have to find out the facts, but you couldn't exactly ask your mates. You couldn't tell on your dad, no matter what he'd done.

Coll knew that every now and then Stuart the policeman would come up to the house and question Dad about this or that. He also knew that some people had a laugh about poaching, like it was a way of getting the better of the toffs who owned all the fishing rights on the river. But how did you know if poaching was bad – or okay really? Coll felt more and more confused as the questions swirled around his mind.

❧ • ❧

They weren't half-way to the beach when Sadie began her usual wailing, 'Wait for me Coll, wait for me.'

'Och wheesht yer nonsense,' he said crossly, striding ahead. He wasn't in the mood for Sadie right now.

At the main road, he called Bracken to heel. 'Sit, lass.' He always made her do this before letting her cross. She was a great dog. Her coat gleamed in the sunshine, a big change from the scruffy-looking puppy she'd been when Dad brought her home from the Rescue kennel. They'd thought at first she was too stupid to train, but here she was a year later, coming to heel, sitting when you told her to, barking when you said 'speak', and no trouble at all. 'Go on then,' he said. She streaked across the road onto the beach, running like a greyhound, her ears blowing in the wind. He followed her down onto the sand, looking to see who was about.

Brakes squealed. A horn blasted. He turned, and

everything went into slow motion. Sadie was halfway across the main road shouting, 'Coll, wait – '

A large van with scratches all over its dirty white paintwork was swerving back and forth out of control, its horn blowing, its driver hanging out of his window bawling abuse at Sadie, his face purple, his bulging bloodshot eyes like those of an enraged bull.

The van bumped sideways into the ditch. The driver burst open the door and leaped out, swearing.

Sadie, who didn't appear to have noticed, skipped down on to the beach. 'Coll, I picked a clover for ye.'

'Aw Sadie!' shouted Coll, angry because he'd got such a shock. 'Can you no' even cross the road right?'

For answer, Sadie presented him with a pink flower. 'Ye can sook at the honey.'

'Go away and gie us peace.' He pushed away the flower, angry and confused. He couldn't be bothered with her, but of course he wouldn't want wee Sadie hurt. If that van had run her over, it would have been his fault.

Sadie trailed away down the beach to where small waves rolled in.

Coll threw a stone at a rusty can and missed. He picked up another one. What if Dad was caught – and jailed? He imagined his father like a crook in a comic, rattling the bars of the Old Jail that was now a tourist attraction in the village.

The sun came out. The tide was halfway in. Farther along the beach, Valentine and Alan were throwing sticks into the sea for Lia. Bracken was prancing in and out of the water, barking at her. Coll felt lonely.

He rather fancied Val, though he'd never dream of telling anyone. He liked her smiley eyes, and the way her goldy-red hair curled down over her shoulders, shining in the sunlight. She wasn't moody, like some girls, and she looked

nice, with her pink cheeks like apples. He didn't want her thinking he was a poacher.

Sadie yelled, 'Val-en-tine!'

Coll cringed. 'Aw shut up, Sadie.' Why did she always have to embarrass him? 'Away and get lost.' But even as he said it he felt guilty. She might have been lying dead, under that van.

Sadie stuck her tongue out at him and ran to meet Valentine and Alan.

Coll hung about, chucking stones at the tin.

As the others came nearer, they'd obviously been talking about him, over Sadie's head. This was going to be difficult, but it had to be faced. He couldn't just turn and run.

Valentine threw a stone and hit his tin.

Coll felt desperate. 'Eh, Lia's paws look okay now.'

'Yes,' said Alan, 'The vet took her bandages off. He said sea water would do her good.'

Coll's brain cleared. Truth was the only option. He blurted out, 'Listen, I cannae be sure – about my Dad, and yon poachers. But I'm no' him. I'm wi' yous about the river. I'm no' wantin' it poisoned.'

Valentine stared at him so long, he felt as if she could see right into his brain, but she spoke to Alan. 'D'you believe him?'

Alan said gently, 'Me and Coll are mates. If he says he's with us, then he is.'

For the first time that day, Coll relaxed. 'Thanks, man.' He felt deeply grateful to his friend.

Sadie swung from Alan and Valentine's hands. 'I'm with yous an' all.' She went on squinting at the bubbles she was blowing with her gum.

A huge man stood yelling down the beach. It was the van driver. He shook his fist. 'You kids is a menace. 'Ow'm I supposed to get outa that?' He pointed furiously at the van tilted sideways in the ditch.

Bracken came running out of the sea. Barking fiercely, sand flying from her feet, she hurled herself at the man, snarling like a lion. The man turned and ran, but not before Bracken had torn off a mouthful of his teeshirt.

'Bracken, get back here!' Coll wondered what had upset her.

The man started clambering into the van, but Lia caught up with Bracken, and the two dogs were shaking the sea-water out of their coats, all over him.

At that moment, Constable Stuart Laurie drew up in his police car. Coll couldn't hear the conversation, but he saw Stuart speaking on his car-phone. When he turned to look at Valentine, her face was white. 'Whit's wrong? Ye look as if ye've seen a ghost.'

'That,' said Valentine, 'is Bloodshot.'

For a while they drifted about on the sand, drawing pictures with sticks. Alan did one of Sadie, with an enormous bubble coming out of her mouth, and Coll tried to do one of Valentine. Sadie drew a dog, and Valentine did one of Bloodshot, with an old toilet brush for his head and a dead jellyfish for a stomach.

When they'd finished, she said, 'Alan, what is the stuff they use to poison rivers anyway?'

'Rabbit gas.'

'Rabbit gas?'

'I've heard Dad talking about it.' Alan aimed another stone at the tin they'd been playing with earlier. This time he hit it.

'That's right,' said Coll. 'The gamies use it tae keep the rabbits down. I've heard my Daddy talkin' about it an' all.'

'Yeah. It's got a name – I forget – something like Cybernet – ' Alan broke off.

'Cybernet – computer talk, Ninja,' scoffed Coll, feeling deeply relieved to be back in favour with his friends.

Alan threw a lump of seaweed at him.

Sadie giggled.

Alan went on mildly, 'The rabbit gas – it's a powder that comes in a tin. The poachers just throw it into the top end of a pool.'

'Aye, but they puncture it first,' said Coll.

Valentine stared at him. How did he know so much about this?

'When the water gets in it makes the powder fizz up like sherbet,' Alan explained, 'but the bubbles are full of poisonous gas. The gas suffocates every living thing in the river – '

Coll wiped the seaweed off his face. 'How come the fish don't poison anyone that eats them?'

'Dad says it's because only their breathing parts – their gills – get damaged. Folk don't eat the gills, so they don't eat the poison.'

'And so' said Valentine 'The poachers can sell the salmon just like – to anyone in the usual way?'

'Yep,' said Alan. 'The trouble is, the poison kills an awful lot of fish. Too many for the poachers' usual sale outlets, like hotels.'

'So that's why they need this refrigerated van,' said Valentine. 'To take the fish where there's more demand – like the town. It all fits.'

Alan picked up the tin he'd hit. 'Hey, look at this.'

Coll peered over his shoulder. Rust streaked what had

once been a green and white label on the tin, but there was no doubt about the word POISON. Sadie squirmed closer for a look. 'No, Sadie,' he said, pulling her away. 'Don't touch.'

Valentine said, 'It's empty. It's been in the sea for ages.' She picked it up. Suddenly she threw it up in the air. 'I know what we can do!'

Coll said, 'What?'

Valentine's eyes met his for a moment, then slid away. 'Oh – nothing.' She kicked the can away.

But Alan persisted, 'Tell us.'

She threw a stone after the can. 'It – um – wasn't any good.'

Coll felt the uncertainty drifting back between them like a barrier. She didn't trust him enough to say her idea in front of him. He wished the ground would swallow him up. He managed to say, 'I won't tell. Anyone.' Would she ever trust him again?

Valentine said, cautiously, 'Well, the first thing we'd need is a rabbit-gas tin – '

'But it's poison,' Alan pointed out. 'All poisons are kept under lock and key.'

Coll wanted more than anything to be part of the plan. 'Supposed to be kept under lock and key. But there's plenty folk that don't bother.'

'Like who?' Alan argued. 'That stuff's really dangerous.'

Coll said 'It's Auld Nick's job tae keep the rabbits down. He's got terrible rabbits up Glen Mellish. He's sure tae have some.'

'That's a lot of use,' objected Alan. 'The gamie isn't exactly going to leave tins full of poison lying about. He'll be like my dad, always locks stuff like that away.'

'We don't need a full tin, stupid,' Valentine snapped.

Alan pointed to where the rusty can bobbed about on a wave. 'What about that one?'

'No,' said Valentine, 'it's got to look new.'

Sadie squeaked, 'Auld Nick throws things on his midden. But no' these tinnies. I've saw where he puts them.'

'Where?' said Valentine, eagerly.

Coll said, 'Tell us, Sadie.'

Sadie looked up at him. 'What'll ye gie me?'

Coll said, 'Och, ye're kiddin'. Whit would a wee scruff like you know.'

Sadie smirked.

Alan dug in his pocket. 'A wee sweetie, Sadie?' He produced a gritty-looking toffee.

Sadie folded her arms and shook her head.

Coll knew that Sadie was thrawn. But bribery did sometimes work. 'A whole packet o' bubblegum, sweetheart?'

Her eyes lit up. 'When?'

'Right after you tell us.'

'Promise?'

'Aye.'

Valentine said persuasively, 'Tell us, Sadie?'

Sadie announced triumphantly 'I've went up tae Auld Nick's lots of times, with my daddy. He puts them in a lobster creel.'

'Aw come on Sadie.' Coll couldn't bear the embarrassment.

'He does. The creel's hangin' on a hook in his shed. He says it's so the doggie doesnae lick at the tinnies.'

Sometimes, Coll had to admit, he could be quite proud of wee Sadie.

Valentine said, 'How could we get one? I don't fancy trying to get past Bounder.'

At last, Coll saw his chance. If he could get hold of one of these tins, it would prove once and for all to his friends that he was on their side. Without stopping to think further, he said, 'I'll away up there now. I'll – watch for Auld Nick goin' out – he'll never go wi'out Bounder. Then – I jooks intae his shed and helps masel'.'

'That shed is always locked,' said Alan. 'I've been up there with my dad too.'

Coll paused. Doubts began to come into his mind, but he fought them back.

Sadie danced up and down. 'I know how tae get in. There's a window at the back o' the shed that's broke. I saw a wee robin flying out it. Auld Nick said it had a nest in there. Maybe there's baby robins now.'

'I'll go,' Coll said quickly. 'I'll go up there – now.' His heart was thumping.

'And me,' said Sadie.

'No, wait,' said Alan. 'Today's no good. Auld Nick could easily be at home. But Dad said something about having a meeting with him and the new summer bailiff he's taken on, late afternoon tomorrow. So you'd know he was – busy.'

'Right, man,' said Coll. 'Tomorrow it is.'

Tuesday

Valentine rushed into the shop before school. Sunlight streamed through the window. Picking up a basket, she took crisps, a carton of juice and two tins of baking-powder.

A small dumpy woman in a pink anorak, flowery mini-skirt and fluorescent orange trainers popped up. 'Hullo, hen.'

'Mrs Munro!'

'You're nice and tall, Val. Can you reach the polish?'

Valentine handed down a can of Pledge.

'Thanks, hen.' She blew her nose on a tiny pink tissue. 'I think I've got a wee summer cold coming on.' The poor little woman looked exhausted, with red rings round her eyes.

Val felt sorry for her. 'You go first.' She stood back to let her past.

'Thanks, hen. I've tae finish the cleanin' at the big house

for the weekend. The toffs are comin'.' Mrs Munro pulled out a pink plastic purse and paid for her shopping.

'You mean the Sheikh?'

'Mr Hassan, yes. And he's bringin' his boy – I've tae make up a bed for him down the stair.'

Valentine took a packet of batteries off the check-out stand. 'He's got kids?' Somehow, she'd never thought of the Sheikh as being quite human before.

'Aye, just the one boy. They say he needs a wheelchair. See ye later, hen.' Mrs Munro waddled out of the shop.

The policeman's mother sat at the checkout.

Valentine plonked her basket on the counter. 'Hi, Mrs Laurie.'

A shadow fell between her and the window, blotting out the sunshine. Concentrating on paying for her shopping, she only noticed a strong smell of cigarettes, sweat and diesel-oil emanating from the new customer. But as she picked up her change, she glanced back. She was staring straight up into the eyes of Bloodshot.

'Packet o' fags, love,' he said to Mrs Laurie, 'an' a four o' Tenants.'

'Please,' said Mrs Laurie. 'Manners don't cost money.'

Somehow Valentine got herself out, almost crashing into Mrs Munro, who had stopped at the kerb, where an empty police car was parked. 'Sorry' Valentine gasped, running across the road. She'd spotted the policeman. 'Mr Laurie – quick!' She grabbed his arm.

He looked surprised. 'Yes?'

She pointed, 'In the shop, that man, he's a p – poacher!'

The policeman grinned slowly and crossed the road towards his car, glancing casually at the shop. 'You'll be done for defamation of character young lady.'

'But I saw him – '

A slight glimmer of interest flickered in the policeman's sleepy eyes, and was quickly extinguished. 'Saw what, exactly?' His voice sounded bored.

'Up at the Salmon Leap on Saturday night. He was – '

'The Salmon Leap? What were you doing, on private property?'

'Nothing – '

At that moment Bloodshot came out of the shop, stripping the plastic loops from a set of lager cans and dropping them on the road.

'That's him!' Valentine whispered, coorying down, forgetting that Bloodshot had never in fact seen her, and so could not possibly recognise her.

Bloodshot was a huge man, his grimy vest wrinkling and stretching over a fat wobbly beer-belly. Valentine saw how he noticed the police car, but walked casually away towards the harbour, pulling the ring out of one of his cans and sucking noisily at the froth. A moment later he disappeared behind his battered white van.

'Why don't you go after him?' Valentine was exasperated. 'Ask him a few questions?'

Constable Laurie smiled. 'Such as what? Er, Mr Thingmy, not only are you a reckless driver, but also this here young lassie says you're a poacher. So how's about I clamp you in irons?' He started his engine. 'Instead, Miss Kerr, perhaps you should explain why you were trespassing up Glen Mellish?'

Why were grown-ups always so patronising? Valentine retorted, 'I haven't time. But,' she allowed her voice to sound cheeky, 'I got a – a recording.'

'Recording?' Obviously he didn't believe her.

'That man said he was going to poison the Mellish. On Friday night.' Anger was getting the better of her. 'And I

taped him.' She had to convince the policeman.

Constable Laurie's voice was softer than ever, 'Quite the wee detective, eh?' He looked casually at the white van as its engine revved, clouds of blue smoke belching from its exhaust.

Valentine said, 'I could play it to you after school.'

'Why not?' Stuart Laurie gave her his sleepy smile and let off the brake. 'I'll be there – unless something unexpected turns up.'

At that moment, the dirty white van drove away. An empty lager can came flying out of the driver's window and clattered along the pavement.

Fingerprints! thought Valentine, running after it, pulling a tissue out of her pocket. Carefully she slid the wrapped can into her poly bag. It stank of beer.

The police car slipped away along the main road. Calmer now, she headed towards school. She'd done what she could. For the time being.

❧ • ☙

By four o'clock Coll had Sadie hidden in the rhododendron bushes at the back of Glenmellish Farm Cottage. Rain was pattering on the leaves and trickling through his hair.

His heart sank; Auld Nick's chimney was smoking, and accordion music blared from a radio. The gamie was at home.

From where Coll crouched, he could see the back door and a line of droopy underclothes dripping on the washing green. A few black hens scratched in the grass. He could also see the hut, surrounded by a thick growth of prickly nettles and thistles. Its door hung squint, fastened with a huge padlock. Not far away, Bounder snored in his kennel, making little woofing noises in his sleep.

'I cannae see a window, Sadie,' he whispered.

'Aye. It's roon the back.'

'What if Bounder wakes up?'

Sadie whispered, 'Bounder knows me. I'll go and play wi' him.'

'He'll eat you alive, Sadie.' Yet how else could he get in to the hut today?

Already, Sadie was creeping out of the bushes. 'Hey, Bounder, nice doggie – '

Bounder leaped from his kennel, barking and growling till he choked to a halt, stopped by his chain.

Coll grabbed Sadie and pulled her back into the bushes. Just in time. Amongst all Bounder's noise, Coll hadn't heard Mr McCrindle's Landrover roaring up the track. It stopped in the yard. The bailiff called 'Mr Nicholas,' and disappeared inside the house.

Two minutes later, a rusty yellow van coughed and spluttered into the yard. Its door creaked as the driver got out – a tall, skinny woman in toffs' gear; wax jacket and green wellies. Her straggly brown hair stuck out from a hat that looked like a cow-pat and her face was wreathed in cigar smoke. Her fingernails were long claws, painted scarlet.

Coll's thoughts moved slowly. 'Who's she, Sadie?' One of the Tuesday fishing syndicate? But fishing tenants had fancy jeeps, or Jaguar cars.

Sadie shrugged.

Bounder growled and showed his teeth at the woman, who edged away towards the back door.

Coll remembered, 'Yon'll be the new summer bailiff.'

The woman walked into the house calling, 'I say, is anyone at home?'

There was no way he was going to get into that hut. Failure stared him in the face. But if he didn't get one of these tins, Valentine would never trust him again.

'I want my tea,' said Sadie.

Valentine laid the tape-recorder on the police-station counter. 'Mrs McCrindle wanted it back. I said I'd forgotten it.'

The policeman had an amused smile on his face. 'Have you mentioned this to bailiff McCrindle? Poachers are more his line.'

'He's never in.' Carefully, Valentine slotted in the new batteries. She pressed 'Play'. The screeching of a million chickens came from the recorder.

'Oh no,' said Valentine. 'What's wrong now?'

'Maybe you touched Fast Forward?' Stuart leaned on one elbow.

She glared at him. She pressed 'Stop'. She pressed 'Play' again. More twittering. She felt like throwing the machine across the room.

'Why don't you just tell me, in your own words?' smiled Stuart.

Anger and frustration got the better of Valentine. Clearly he still didn't believe her. And now she could see other difficulties. How much information could she actually give, without implicating Coll? How did she know Stuart wouldn't go telling her mother? Bursting into tears, she grabbed the recorder and ran.

Veils of grey drizzle hung over the sea-loch as Valentine went trailing along the beach. For the second time, she'd failed to deliver the evidence about Bloodshot's plan. She only had three days left, to stop the poisoning of the river. Three days till Friday. She was beginning to wonder if she'd dreamed it all. No-one else seemed to care.

FORM was supposed to be doing a beach clean-up. But only Alan was there, skimming flat stones across the water. 'Where is everyone?' she called.

'You're late,' he said. 'They said it was too wet. They've gone home. I was just going, myself.'

She told him what had happened, then said, 'We could do the bridge. It'd be dry there.'

'Okay. But not for long. I want to get the newsletter into the computer.'

It was dark under the bridge, as they began clearing the rubbish, and disgustingly smelly. Every now and then a car or a lorry would rumble over, shaking the old stone structure. Green slime and mud slithered down.

'Hey, look at this.' Alan picked up an old boot and pushed his hand in, making the sole flap like a mouth. 'Ma saying "good-morning children".'

Valentine laughed, feeling calmer.

'Val, you said you'd a brilliant idea?'

She outlined her plan.

Alan bundled a mess of old fishing line and scraps of polythene into his black bag, 'That's clever. But everything depends on Coll getting that empty tin.'

'Hey, wait a minute, said Valentine. 'What's this?' Three fat black bin-bags, stashed in a corner.

Alan sloshed through the river to where she stood. The bags were tightly tied. He felt each of them. 'Didn't you say Bloodshot – '

'Was to dump the gear here for Mr Munro.' Valentine's heart was thumping. 'This proves I wasn't imagining everything.'

'Hang on,' he said, tearing a small hole in the plastic. 'This way, we'll know for sure.' He thrust his hand in and pulled out a neat roll of netting. 'Whew. It looks like you were right. Now what do we do?'

Valentine's mind was racing. 'What if your dad could catch them picking this up?'

'Yes, but – when was Davy to collect it?'

'Tonight – Tuesday. And Fanshawe was to hand over the poison.'

'No good. Dad's at a meeting, then he's away over to Loch Fyne till late.'

Valentine bit her thumb, thinking hard. 'And I've got to be home for tea-time, or I won't be allowed out again.'

Mrs Kerr's mind was elsewhere. 'Val, all the salmon in the next loch have had to be slaughtered. This horrible new fish disease – it's awful. And I don't know exactly what signs to look for – disease is more Dad's line.'

'Phone him?' said Valentine. 'And he'll be home Friday night. Um – is it okay if I go out after tea, Mum?'

'It's your turn to clear up. Where are you going?' Mum sounded nervous.

'To meet Alan. To – er – finish our clean-up.' Valentine pointed to the village across the bay. 'You'll be able to see us.'

'The shop. That reminds me – baking powder?'

'The new tin's in the cupboard. You owe me.'

'Thanks, Val.'

The phone rang. Mrs Kerr picked it up. 'Dishes first. And don't be late. Oh hi, Mary.'

While Val washed up, her mother mourned down the phone; 'All the other fish-farms keep diseases at bay by swilling chemicals into their cages . . . No, we can't. We're trying to grow organic salmon as good as wild fish. It's bad enough about the feed . . . Well, it's supposed to be ground-up fish protein, but of course the manufacturers never say exactly what's in it, and the pink colouring's always chemical . . . No, quite. Who wants to be putting a lot of poison into the water?'

At the word 'poison', Valentine grabbed her jacket and ran.

꩜ • ꩜

Coll sat in the kitchen looking at his tea. He wasn't hungry. Opposite him wee Sadie had almost finished her plateful of sausage and beans on toast.

'If you're no' wantin' that,' said his father, 'I'll take it.'

The fat was congealing on the sausages. As Coll stared at them, an idea began to wriggle its way into his mind like a fish swimming upstream against the current.

'I do want it,' he said, beginning slowly to fork beans into his mouth, thinking hard.

His father got up. 'I'll be away then.'

'Okay' said Coll, trying not to let his father interrupt his train of thought.

'Where are ye goin', Daddy?' piped wee Sadie.

'You're that nosy,' said her father. 'I'm just goin' – out. Coll, you mind Sadie till your mammy gets back. She'll be in soon.'

With no-one else to confide in, Coll spent the next hour

lying around on the floor, his head on Bracken's flank, telling his idea to Sadie. He finished, 'So, you'll tell the teacher I'm sick, right?'

☙ • ❧

In the darkening bus-shelter at the edge of the village, Valentine felt cold. The street-lights had come on and only a couple of boys were still fishing off the end of the pier.

Alan got up, 'I'm away home. Nothing's happening.'

'Listen!'

The rattle of a motorbike engine. A light-beam, wobbling along. The bike slewed in to the lay-by, backfiring loudly, and stopped.

Valentine pulled Alan down. 'Mr Munro's Yamaha!'

'He'll never get the bags onto that,' said Alan.

Another light cut the gloom, approaching from the estate. This time it was a yellowish van with only one headlamp. It parked beside the motorbike.

'Who's that?' said Valentine.

Mr Munro and the lanky van-driver clambered under the bridge. They reappeared, heaving one of the black bags. Looking around, they pushed it into the van. They went back for another, puffing and panting with the effort.

On the far side of the bay a string of traffic crawled towards them, slowed by the late-night bus.

The bus came over the bridge just as the last bag was shoved into the van. It drew in at the lay-by, hiding the van, the people, the Yamaha and the bus shelter from the queue of vehicles which now drove past. The last one to pass was the McCrindle Land-rover.

'Nice one, Dad,' sighed Alan. 'You've just missed seeing the poachers. In action.'

65

In the silence left after the bus had departed, the thin van-driver's voice sounded sharp as a razor. 'I say, that was a close shave.'

Mr Munro said, 'Where's the stuff?'

'The poison, you mean? Wot's the hurry, old boy?'

'Only three days. When –?'

'Tomorrow. Mr Nicholas is awf to Lochgilphead, and I've got a half-day. The stuff's in his hut, in a locked box.' She jingled some keys. 'These were hanging on a hook at his back door. I took them after the meeting. Clever, wot?' Her cackling laugh ended with a coughing fit.

The Yahama revved. The van followed it into the dark.

Wednesday Morning

Alan pressed the 'Print' button on the computer. He checked the clock at the bottom of the screen. Eight fifteen. Plenty of time before school.

Mrs McCrindle came in with a fried egg roll. 'Nearly done?' The printer rolled out twenty copies of 'Friends Of the River Mellish Newsletter no. 1'. She picked one up. 'This looks great.'

'Mmm, not bad.' Hungry now, Alan crammed the warm roll into his mouth.

'Thank goodness you can operate this thing, Alan. Dad gets so cross.'

'Maybe I'll work with computers, when I grow up.' Alan wiped egg-yolk off his chin and licked flour grains from his hand.

'Maybe you should.' His mother picked up her briefcase. 'I've got an hour on the river after school – I'm taking Valentine, you too, if you want – '

'No thanks, Mum.'

'Don't be long.'

Alan began switching off the computer. It was a great machine. He was hopeless at football and shinty. And most of the boys didn't seem to like him.

Valentine, frank as ever, once explained, 'It's because you're the teacher's son. They think you'll go telling on them, after school.'

Coll, his one loyal friend, had said, 'And you're the bailiff's son. That's as bad as havin' a polisman for yer daddy.' Occasionally Coll came and played computer games with him, though Alan usually won.

He slid the newsletters into his bag. If he was quick, he'd catch Coll on the way to school and find out if he'd managed to get the tin from Auld Nick's hut last night.

❦

Coll was stuffing various items into his pockets, shouting, 'C'mon, Sadie, time tae go.'

As arranged, Sadie came running from the kitchen. 'Cheerio Mammy, Daddy,' she sang, like a child-actor in a TV soap. 'Have a nice day.' She never normally said anything when she went out.

Coll gave Bracken the last of his bread. 'Stay,' he said. She watched him go, her eyes wistful.

By the time he reached the fork in the road, Sadie reverted to her normal character, pestering him. 'Aw Coll, take me wi' ye?'

'No.'

'Why no'?'

'Och Sadie, you're tae tell the teacher I'm no weel.'

'Aye, but – '

From here, the narrow tarmac road led down to the village, and school. The unused grassy track led over the ruined bridge, up the hill to Glenmellish Farm, and Auld Nick's house.

Coll waved his hand in the direction of school. 'Go on, Sadie.'

She stood her ground. 'I could tell the teacher whaur ye really are.'

'Ye wouldnae.'

'I might.' Her blue eyes looked huge, gazing up at him. 'Though I wouldnae want tae get ye intae any bother, nor nothin'.' She smiled sweetly.

Coll felt his resolve crumbling, 'I'll buy ye loads o' bubble-gum.'

She glared at him, 'Ye've nae money.'

'Sadie, please.'

She sighed dramatically. 'Oh a'right.' Giving him a cheeky sideways look, she trailed slowly away down the road in the direction of school, her bag bumping along the road, her head lolling from side to side as she sang, '*In and out the dusty bluebells* – '

Coll watched, half cross, half laughing, till she was out of sight. What a lassie. He set off at a steady run, his footsteps scattering droplets of water from the wet grasses.

Half an hour later, he was watching Auld Nick's house. No smoke came from the chimney today, but Bounder still lay sleeping in his kennel. The hens clucked peacefully beneath the droopy washing.

The back-door latch clicked. Auld Nick came out with a gun under his arm. Bounder woke up and stretched, showing his huge claws. Ears up, he slouched out of his kennel looking hopeful, his chain clanking. Auld Nick went striding off up the hill without him. Bounder lifted his leg against the washing pole and slunk back into his kennel. He flopped his head down onto his paws, looking fed-up.

A steady drizzle began. Coll could hear his own heart thumping. He unwrapped two cold sausages. Holding one out towards Bounder, he advanced on the kennel.

The dog sat up, sniffing at the sausage. He took it carefully, enormous teeth gleaming under his soft jowls. While he munched, Coll grabbed the gamie's dripping long-johns off the washing line. Two clothes pegs shot into the air. As Bounder began to chew at the second sausage, Coll slipped the garment over his nose the way he'd seen Mrs McCrindle muzzle Lia last week. He tied the legs of the long-johns firmly above Bounder's ears. The dog tried to bark, but only a muffled 'woof' came through the thick wool.

Coll heard a giggle from the bushes.

'Sadie!'

His wee sister crawled out. 'Hee, hee, Bounder looks like he's got the toothache.'

'Sadie, you're supposed tae be at the school.' He was mad at her.

'I follied you a' the way and ye never heard me,' she stuck her tongue out at him.

There was no time to argue. Auld Nick might not have gone far and Bounder was already pawing at his big head, trying to get rid of his makeshift muzzle.

'You wait there, Sadie. And haud yer wheesht. I'll be right back.'

He ran across the yard. He tried the hut door, but it was firmly padlocked. He went round to the back. There was the window, one pane broken. But it was far too small for

him to squeeze through.

He peered inside. He could just make out the old lobster-pot, hanging from the rafters.

Sadie clutched his sleeve, 'I'll can get in. I'm wee enough.'

'I told ye to stay in the bushes.'

But Sadie was already swarming up his legs. 'Bend over, till I staun on yer rump. Quick.'

Coll laid his damp jacket over the jaggy glass. 'Mind, it's cutty.' He bent. Her feet dug into his spine. Then her weight was off him. He stood up. Most of Sadie was inside the window.

'There's a bench. Gie my legs a wee shove' came her voice.

He pushed at her legs. There was a crash, followed by a small squeal.

'Can ye see the lobster creel?' he called softly.

'It's awfy high up. Oh, Coll,' squeaked Sadie, 'It's fu' o' tinnies, right enough.'

'Great,' said Coll. 'Gie it a dunt wi' a brush or somethin', so they spill out. Whistle when ye've got one.'

Coll fled to the rhododendrons. Time passed. Several thumps came from the hut and, at last, a faint whistle. He was halfway across the yard, running, when he heard the splash of tyres, and an engine.

'Someone's comin' Sadie.'

'Oh no,' came Sadie's wail. 'The bench's legs have broke. I cannae reach the windie.'

'Coorie doon, till they're awa'. I'll jook back into the bushes.'

The rusty yellow van parked close to the hut door. The driver pulled a bunch of keys from her pocket and began scrabbling at the padlock with her scarlet claws.

Alan McCrindle put plates on the table. There was something companionable and cosy about Dad making lunch. Today there was tomato soup and thick cheese sandwiches.

Dad poured the soup into two mugs. 'I'll be needing your help on the computer again.'

'What for?'

'D'you know how to send an e-mail?'

'You do it on the Internet,' Alan dipped his sandwich into his soup, 'We're connected okay.'

'It's all gobbledigook to me. Tonight, then?'

Alan sank his teeth into the soft bread. The sharp saltiness of the cheese brought saliva rushing into his mouth. 'I might have to – see Coll.'

'And how are all your pals this weather?'

'The Munros weren't at school.' Alan felt a bit worried. Could something have gone wrong with Coll's plan?

His father put the kettle on. They ate in friendly silence. On impulse Alan said, 'Is it true that Coll's dad is a poacher?'

His father stopped eating. 'What?'

'Well, they're all saying Mr Munro's in some big poaching gang.'

'Who's 'all'?'

'Valentine Kerr.'

'What does that lassie know about Ardmellish ways, and her only here a few months? Och Davy'll maybe take a fish from the river now and then, for their dinner. But he'd never – '

'Is that not poaching?'

'Well, yes – and no. There's a tradition; taking a wee fish for the pot isn't such a crime. It's different if folk start trying to sell their catch, but Davy would never do that.'

'Wouldn't he?'

'No way. The Sheikh's that nervous the locals might take
a fish, he's closed the estate to everyone except his paid-up
ticket holders. But, to me, there's give and take. Davy Munro
knows the estate, and the folks from hereabout. He'd soon
let us know if he'd seen any yobs about.'

'Would he?'

'He would that. You know, some of these neds think
nothing of giving legitimate fishers a doing. Then we get
the complaints; "Where was the bailiff?" I can't be
everywhere at the one time. It's a help to me that Davy's
taking a wee walk up the river now and then. Davy Munro's
a straight man.'

Alan bit into another sandwich. 'But there's this guy Val
saw – '

'Valentine Kerr again? Listen, son. When you get back to
school, tell madam Kerr I'll be taking care of any poachers
in Glen Mellish.' His father looked at him sternly. 'Poachers
are dangerous. Right?'

'Okay.' Alan had been going to tell him about Valentine's
recording, but there was no point when Dad was in this
mood. He'd wait till after the computer session tonight. He
got up. 'I'd better get back to school.'

☙ • ❧

Coll sat hunched on the floor of the caravan, staring at his
feet, wishing he was at school with his mates. What a mess
he'd got Sadie into.

Sadie perched on the seat, gazing out of the grimy
window, singing a lullaby to the lumpy-looking dolly she
cradled in her arms. *'In and out the dusty bluebells – '* Her
wee pink nose was running with green snot and her cheeks
were covered in raspberry jam.

Coll felt as if he was going through a nightmare. It had been terrible, watching helplessly while the skinny dame unlocked the hut, hearing her scrabbling about inside, wondering if Sadie would manage to stay hidden, then seeing Sadie being dragged squealing out of the hut clutching her dolly, shoved into van and the door slammed shut.

He had come out of the bushes running. Next thing, the woman's fingernails were clawing at his neck, half-throttling him, as she shoved him into the back of the van and locked the door.

Through the rear window, he'd seen her run to Auld Nick's house, the hut keys jangling. She came back without them. She'd driven the two of them up here to the quarry and marched them into this manky caravan, which stank of stale smoke. The minute they were in, she'd turned the key in the lock and stuck it down her welly boot.

She'd lit a cigar. She breathed the smoke out of her nostrils, like a dragon. She'd started trying to sweeten them up, feeding them pieces and jam, trying to persuade them they were all three sharing this great secret.

Now she stood over them, her red talons curved round another cigar, her hand shaking slightly. The fumes were making Coll's brain sleepy. She was turning nasty. 'I say, p'rhaps I should just hand you over to Mr Nicholas. He'll be very interested to hear what you were up to in his hut.'

Sadie turned her eyes on. 'My dolly's goin' tae tell Auld Nick you wis stealin' his rabbit-gas.'

'Shut it, Sadie,' Coll spoke through his teeth.

The thin woman smiled unpleasantly. 'Darling child. That's my job. My boss – Mr McCrackers or wotever he's called – said I'd to use my initiative, as the new seasonal bailiff.' Then she gritted her teeth and spat out an inch of cigar she'd bitten off by mistake. 'And wot I do is no business of a couple of little creeps like you. Who are you, anyway?'

Somewhere far away, Bounder was baying. He must have got his muzzle off at last. The eerie sound echoed up the glen. Then came a shot.

It wasn't the shooting season yet, thought Coll. He wished he hadn't tied Bounder up. He tried imagining how Bounder would have chased this dame but, right now, his fuddled brain couldn't deal with what was going on. Right now, he had to dream up a way to get himself and Sadie out of this. And he hadn't an idea in his head.

Sadie was sliding off the seat wriggling about in an exaggerated way.

The thin woman looked surprised. 'Wot's up with you?'

'Oh, oh, I need the toilet,' Sadie was doing her best whine, while rolling her eyes at Coll. 'I need it – now!'

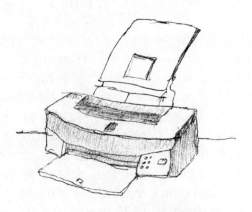

Wednesday Afternoon

After school, Alan went home to take Lia out. He headed for the Munro's.

He knocked at the door. 'Anyone in? Coll?'

Inside, a chair scraped on the kitchen floor. Davy Munro came out. 'Hullo there. Coll's no' back from the school yet.'

Alan twisted his fingers together. 'Oh, right.' Everything was getting too difficult. If Davy Munro was involved in the poaching plot, how could Alan explain Coll might be in some sort of trouble through trying to stop it? But, if Coll and Sadie were in trouble, how could he not tell their father what he knew?

Bracken poked her head out. She liked playing with Lia and they often went for walks together.

An idea came into Alan's head. 'Er, maybe I'll go and meet them, Mr Munro. Can I take Bracken?' His idea was that Bracken might help find his friends, wherever they were.

Mr Munro handed him a leather lead. 'Aye, if she'll go wi' you. Here, you'll need this. You cannae trust her near sheep.'

Alan clipped the lead to Bracken's collar. 'Come on, lass.' The big dog looked slightly surprised, her eyes moving from Davy to Alan, but she went along with him willingly enough.

As soon as he was round the corner, Alan unleashed her. There were no sheep down here near the river. Bracken frisked about at first, delighted to be free. She wanted Lia to play with her, and pranced around her, teasingly. Lia looked up at him, not understanding why she wasn't being freed too. 'Bracken,' he called, 'Where's Sadie? Go and find Sadie!'

She looked up at him, her head on one side, then raced off, nose to the ground. She could move like the wind, thanks to her greyhound blood. Had she understood what he said? He followed her, running, not wanting to lose sight of her, through the wood, over the ruined bridge. Seconds later, she disappeared up the path, heading for Auld Nick's cottage.

He wished Valentine was here. Two brains were better than one, and she was no fool. But right now she was fishing with his mother. He sped onwards.

Valentine yelled, 'Help! I've caught a fish!'

The fishing line quivered against her finger as if it was electric. The end of her rod flexed and curved, gleaming like a live thing in the late afternoon sunshine. 'What do I do?'

The teacher came running. 'Great! You haven't caught him yet, though. Easy does it. Let him run a bit, give him some line, that's right.'

Valentine couldn't believe the strength of the fish. She could see nothing in the dark mysterious pool, yet her line zoomed about all over the pool, making a shining V-shaped wake. 'It must be huge!'

'Keep your rod up,' said Mrs McCrindle, 'and concentrate.'

Valentine's reel screamed as the fish pulled out line, streaking to the far end of the pool, where the river spilled away into shallow rapids. Her rod throbbed with the energy of it.

'He'll come back,' said the teacher. 'Wait.'

Valentine felt the line slacken as, sure enough, the fish turned at the shallows. Flagging, it swam more slowly back up towards the deep water beneath the waterfall. Her arm ached with tiredness, but the fish wasn't giving in yet. The line thrummed.

'Keep your mind on the job, girl! Rod up and – hold the line tight! I'll fetch the landing net.'

Silver scales glinted just below the surface. 'Oh look!' whispered Valentine. Now she'd actually seen her fish, half of her felt sorry for him. But half couldn't wait to land him.

Suddenly the end of her line came clean out of the water. There was nothing on it, not even the fly. All that was left on the smooth surface was a swirl of bubbles.

'Oh no! It got away!'

'It did,' Mrs McCrindle picked up the empty bag and the landing net. 'And so do most of them.'

'What did I do wrong?'

'Nothing. Actually, you did really well to get into a fish your first time on the river. Not many people are that lucky.'

'Can I try again?'

'Sorry, Valentine. My time's up. I've a meeting after tea, and huge piles of admin to do. Can't put it off – Gavin wants me out on poacher-watch this weekend. Let's hope Mr Nicholas has another "empty" day next week.'

Valentine started taking down her rod. Imagine having a salmon on the end of your line, and letting it get away. 'How big was my fish?'

'Somewhere between two and three pounds, maybe.'

Valentine didn't want the teacher to see her disappointment, so changed the subject. 'Can salmon really jump up waterfalls?'

'Certainly. I've often seen them here. Soon, now, lots will arrive from the sea. They'll wait in the lie at the foot of the waterfall there, and when the water feels right, they'll start leaping. They have to get upriver to spawn.'

'Um – thankyou, Mrs McCrindle. Sorry I didn't catch that salmon.'

'Cheer up. You fished well. Now, come along.'

When they reached the main road, Mrs McCrindle let her out of the car. 'By the way, you've no idea what's up with the Munro children? It's unlike both of them to be off school at the same time.'

Valentine shook her head.

Mrs McCrindle looked at her for a moment. 'See you in the morning then.'

Valentine set off along the road, anxiety about Coll now uppermost in her mind. Was he in trouble – because of her daft idea? Obviously her plan was a total failure – without a look-alike poison tin, there was no way she could make it work.

The red post-van passed. Lachy leaned out. 'Like a lift? I've mail for your fish farm, after I've done the estate deliveries.'

'Yes, please.'

❦ • ❧

Opposite Auld Nick's house, Alan crawled through the bushes. There was no-one about. 'Stay, Lia.' She lay down, watching him intently.

Near the hut, Bracken was bouncing round Bounder, who seemed to have trampled some of Auld Nick's washing into the mud by his kennel. His chain clanked as he tried to play with her. Away up the hill a sheep bleated.

Alan's hand stuck to something soft. Ugh, someone's spat-out splodge of pink bubblegum. He scraped it off with a stick. Sadie! She was always chewing the stuff. 'Bracken, go find Sadie.'

Bracken weaved back and forth across the yard. She snuffled excitedly at the shed door, which hung open, then she bounded inside and began to bark.

Alan sprinted to the hut. Bracken crashed about. She leaped on a broken bench by the window, knocking over an old lobster pot. She rushed outside. Alan followed. But not until he'd read the squiggly writing on the unbroken window, 'Sabie Mun'.

'Lia, come.' He ran after Bracken, who was heading for the old quarry.

Lachy's post-van came up the road. 'My, you're in a hurry, son. I've a friend o' yours here.'

Valentine got out. 'Thanks for the lift, Lachy. I'll walk from here.'

Lachy waved. 'Any time. I'll away – second-last delivery of the day and it has to be that lassie Fanshawe, with her hoity toity voice and never even a cup of tea.' He drove off.

Alan was already running. 'Hurry, Val. Bracken's disappeared.' He panted out his explanation. He definitely wasn't fit.

Lachy drove past them on his way down the road. 'Nobody at home' he called. 'And no letter box. Typical.'

When Alan reached the crest of the hill, Bracken was nowhere to be seen. There was only brown moorland dotted with grey sheep and white lambs.

A shot rang out. The echo repeated round the encircling hills; bang, bang, bang. Then silence crept back.

Inside the caravan, the thin woman removed her claws from where she'd clamped them over Coll's face.

Coll wished Lachy had forced the door open, instead of just shouting rude words. Though they had been funny. He rubbed his sore face. He was worried about Sadie. How would she get home? She was only wee. If she was in danger, then it was his fault. But she was a right clever lassie, escaping like that.

The woman had let Sadie take the key from her welly to unlock the door. Sadie was to go out and pee in the quarry, and she'd get sweeties when she came back. Coll had never known Sadie resist sweeties before.

He heard a shot.

Valentine had never been up to the quarry before. It was overgrown with thickets of prickly gorse bushes blooming yellow. An old white caravan sat among them. Beside it was the rusty vehicle she'd seen last night. Of course – Fanshawe.

At that point, Auld Nick staggered over the skyline, carrying a big brown animal. 'Did you let this dog loose up here?' he yelled aggressively at Alan.

Valentine recognised Bracken. Blood poured down.

'What happened?'

'This dog was out of control, chasing the sheep all over the place, and their lambs. If I hadn't put a bullet through her, she'd have attacked one of them. The farmer would have had her destroyed.'

Valentine felt sick. 'Oh, poor Bracken. Is she – dead?'

Alan's face was ashen, but he faced the gamekeeper. 'It's my fault, Mr Nicholas.' He tried to explain everything, finishing, 'She just – took off – '

Valentine reached out to stroke Bracken's head. There was the faintest movement in her tail. 'Oh, look. She's alive. It's her back leg that's hurt.'

'Aye,' said the gamekeeper. 'She was moving that fast I nearly missed her. She's lucky. There's not much I miss on this hill.'

Bracken opened her eyes and gazed soulfully at Valentine. She began to whine softly, but her voice was drowned by the sound of the McCrindle Landrover arriving.

'Good-day to you, Mr Nicholas,' called the bailiff. 'Would you have seen the Munro lad hereabouts?'

'If I could get my hands on him. This here's his dog.' The gamekeeper went on to tell what had happened. 'I doubt she'll not be going after sheep again.'

Mr McCrindle said, 'I found the wee lass. She said she was lost, and oh, the tears on her. Isn't that right Sadie?'

Sadie's tear-stained face looked out of the side window.

The bailiff went on, 'She says her brother's in the caravan.' He went to knock on the caravan door. 'I'll have a wee word with Miss Fanshawe.'

Relief swept over Valentine. Wee Sadie was safe.

Fanshawe's head appeared, grinning like a skull, surrounded in smoke from her cigar. She shoved Coll out in front of her as if she was pulling a rabbit from a hat. 'I say, Mr McCrindle, I caught these kids vandalising Mr Nicholas's hut. One ran awf.'

'Ah, I thought they must have been up to something.'

'Indeedy. That one,' she pointed a bony finger at Sadie, 'lied. Told me her dolly fell into Mr Nicholas's shed, and her brother pushed her in the window – wich I noticed they'd broken.'

'Very observant, Miss Fanshawe. Thank you. I'll return them to their parents, who will doubtless be dealing with them.' Mr McCrindle led Coll to the Landrover.

Valentine thought Coll looked awful as he clambered in beside her.

Mr McCrindle was saying, 'I'm afraid your dog's had a bit of an accident, Coll.' He lifted Bracken out of Auld Nick's arms. 'Now, let's take a look at this leg.' He laid her on some sacks beside Coll. 'Hmm. It looks pretty bad. She'll need the vet right away. We'll drop her at the surgery.'

Valentine's heart bled for Coll. He was staring at his dog, his face white.

'Good day to you, Mr Nicholas.' Mr McCrindle started up the Landrover.

The gamekeeper went striding off down the hill, shaking his head.

Coll put his arms round Bracken and burst into tears.

Alan, sitting with Lia, confessed to Coll why he'd brought Bracken and how well she'd tracked them.

Coll wiped his face on his sleeve. 'Will she be all right?'

The bailiff looked round. 'That leg'll take time to heal, and she'll be weak, for she's lost a lot of blood. But she's a fine healthy young dog, that's been well cared for in recent times – and the vet's very good.'

Coll curled his body round Bracken, protecting her from the bumps as they swerved down the road.

Sadie cradled her doll, crooning a little song. It was made from pieces of sacking and had a lumpy tummy. She'd drawn big eyes and a smile on its face with charcoal. Bits of straw stuck out from its head and it wore a wee blue plastic flower-pot for a hat, with a yellow dandelion drooping from the hole at the top. Suddenly, she handed the doll to Valentine.

'What's its name, Sadie?' Valentine pretended to rock it in her arms.

'Poison,' said Sadie, gazing up at Valentine out of clear blue eyes. 'You've to keep her. You're her mummy now.'

'Poison? That's a funny name for a dolly,' said Alan.

'Some people are dozy dumplings, aren't they Sadie?' said Valentine, and the two girls began to giggle.

Alan shrugged at Coll. 'Women.'

Coll said, 'Och Sadie's been nursin' that rubbishy thing a' afternoon. She wouldnae leave it behind.'

But later, Valentine thought she heard Coll whispering to his little sister, 'You're pure brilliant, wee Sadie.' So maybe he wasn't so stupid, after all.

Later that evening, when Alan got back from the vet's, he found his father red in the face with rage, staring at the computer's blue screen as though expecting to see visions therein.

'Thank goodness you're back, son. I'm going mad here! I must get this e-mail to the Sheikh. Look, here's the 'send' button. But when I press it a menu comes up 'Delete all data?' And whether I press 'yes' or 'no' it says 'You have performed an illegal operation.' What am I supposed to do?'

Alan sat down at the keyboard. 'It's quite simple, Dad', he said, getting on with sending the e-mail. And it was only because he was tired that he didn't think of asking Dad what he was contacting the Sheikh about.

Thursday

Valentine's morning started badly. Hoping for warm toast and a bit of helpful chat, she found Mum stabbing the telephone buttons as if poking out the eyes of her worst enemy. 'Hullo? Hullo. Ardmellish Fish Farm here. Where's our order? You were supposed to deliver smolts on Monday . . . Well, make sure it *is* today.' She slammed the phone down, glaring at her daughter. 'You're late, Valentine. Again.'

Valentine knew there was no point in trying to talk. She made herself a sandwich and picked up her schoolbag.

Her mother's parting shot was 'Home by teatime. That room of yours is a disgrace. It's to be cleaned before your father comes back tomorrow.'

Not that Dad would notice, thought Valentine. How she wished he was here, with his quiet, sensible ways.

She trudged along the beach chewing her dry sandwich,

thinking. One, could she now depend on Coll? Two, how could she make the next part of her plan work?

Last night, everything had seemed so great. The moment she got home, she'd dashed upstairs to untie Sadie's 'doll'. Inside she found, as she expected, an empty poison tin, its green and white label as fresh as new. Carefully, she'd filled it with baking powder, hidden in her pillowcase since Tuesday. It was in her pocket now.

But how was her spoof tin to be substituted for the real thing? If she failed to do this, tomorrow night her beloved river would be ruined by Bloodshot and his gang.

Her wellies slithered over the river's stony outflow. Through the road-bridge she could see the big house, sitting on its wide lawns. It looked empty and unloved. There seemed something wrong, that the Sheikh was so rich he could own a huge estate and not even bother living there, while locals like the Munros, who'd loved and cared for it all their lives, had to be so poor. Maybe, if she was Mr Munro, she'd be angry enough to hit back at the Sheikh, too. But not by poisoning the river.

She thought over the facts so far; the poachers' bags had been taken from under the bridge on Tuesday night. Where were they now? Wee Sadie had seen Fanshawe stealing rabbit-gas from a locked cupboard in Auld Nick's hut. Where was it now? If only she knew, she'd find a way to do the swap.

There were so many ifs. If Coll was truly against the poachers, she could ask him to search for the bags. Quite likely they'd be hidden somewhere near his house. But if he was working with the poachers, she'd simply be giving the game away. Confusion racked her brain.

Coll sat on the playground wall, staring at his feet.

She walked into the school without speaking to him.

All morning Coll stared out of the classroom window. He watched the tide begin to come in, lifting the dry seaweed like hair and swirling it about. Oyster-catchers strutted on their red legs, whistling to each other. It must be great to be a bird, free as air, with none of the complications boys had to suffer. He wished he could be outside in the sunshine. Problems were easier sorted out of doors.

Mrs McCrindle kept annoying him. 'What's your answer, Coll?'

'I wisnae here, yesterday.'

'And so far,' she said crisply, 'I haven't seen a note from your mother.'

Round and round went his brain, going over yesterday. Sadie in Fanshawe's caravan, playing with her dolly. His beloved Bracken with her leg all blood, the vet giving her an injection to make her sleep, setting the broken leg-bone and making a fibreglass stookie for it. Mum crying in the police car because her bairns had gone missing. And now the worst blow of the lot.

Just as he left for school this morning, Dad said, 'Ye'll be workin' wi me tomorrow night, son, so don't go makin' any dates with your pals, right?'

'What's on, Daddy?'

'Never you mind. There's a – a job tae be done, and I'll be needin' you. That's a' ye have tae know, right?'

His heart sinking, Coll knew this could mean only one thing. He was to go with the poachers. He was to help them poison the Mellish.

How would he ever be able to look his friends in the face again? He felt terrible.

Valentine went along to the shop for her lunch. Mrs Munro stood at the checkout clutching a fluorescent yellow toy, and weeping.

Mrs Laurie's hand was on her arm. 'Och Maddy, cheer up. Your bairns are safe now.'

Mrs Munro sniffed, 'It was terrible, not knowin' where they were.'

'Aye, and you wouldn't know whether to give them a skelp or a hug when they got home.'

Valentine desperately wanted to say sorry to Mrs Munro – but daren't divulge the plan which had caused Sadie to have such a scary experience. She should have gone up to Auld Nick's herself.

Mrs Munro sobbed, 'I got my giro the day. Sadie's wee bird wouldnae flap its wings right.' She pressed the beak of the plastic duck. One wing went up and down weakly. 'She's been on about batteries for weeks. I'm that glad to hae her safe, I'd buy her the moon if I could.'

'Here's your batteries.' Mrs Laurie undid the packet helpfully.

'I cannae see where they're supposed to go.' Mrs Munro handed the duck to Valentine.

Valentine opened the duck's tummy, slid out the old batteries and fitted in the new ones.

'Thanks, hen.' Mrs Munro said. 'You're a good friend tae my bairns. Sadie thinks the world o' you.'

Valentine felt as if a knife twisted in her heart. Unthinkingly she slid the used batteries into her pocket and paid for her chocolate.

Outside, a chill ran down her spine. The yellow van was parking. Fanshawe loped into the shop, her voice neighing, 'I say, do *you* stock Havana thins heah? I've tried everywere.'

The van was thick with dirt. Valentine sauntered round it. Her finger wrote 'Do not disturb. Seeds planted.' She reached for the back door. It creaked open. There sat the black bags! She pulled the tin from her pocket and stuffed it in the hole Alan had torn.

A stream of grey cigar smoke belched from the shop, followed by Fanshawe, coughing.

Quick! No time to search for Fanshawe's tin. Valentine

dodged across the road and jumped down onto the beach. Trying to look casual, she kicked an empty beer can along.

Fanshawe's beaky nose hung over the sea-wall. 'I say, child. Were you vandalisin' my cah?'

Valentine's eyes practically fell out of their sockets, but she made her voice sound bored. 'It was that boy.' She tipped her head towards the shop.

Fanshawe craned her neck, like a crow, searching for the non-existent boy.

Valentine took to her heels along the beach, laughing. She ran along the edge of the incoming tide, not caring if the spray washed into her wellies, singing at the top of her voice. She'd done it, she'd done it! And without help from Coll or anyone. A great wave of energy and delight surged through her.

Alan was beside her for the afternoon. She scribbled him a note, 'The dummy's planted,' feeling pleased when she saw the surprise on his face. He mouthed 'How?' And she shrugged as though to say 'no problem'.

Mrs McCrindle picked up the note, 'Shall we share this?' She dropped it in the bin. 'Silly people. Now, Valentine, how did your FORM interviews go last Saturday?'

Valentine had almost forgotten about the survey she'd been doing. Everyone else had refused to interview grown-ups, but she wasn't shy. Being an only child she was used to older people, in fact she found them interesting.

Now, while she explained about the flat batteries, a thought gathered in her head. 'Will it be all right if I give the tape recorder to Alan later?'

'Very well. But don't forget. It's school property.'

As the afternoon wore on, Valentine's elation evaporated. It was true she had succeeded in delivering her tin of substitute poison. But Fanshawe had the real stuff too.

❧ • ❧

After school she hung out with Alan down by the pier. The tide was full in, sunshine glinting on the calm surface. Two men were unloading boxes of prawns from their boat. The fish lorry waited by the pier. The air smelt of salty things, tar and fish.

She dug the tape-recorder out of her bag and gave it to Alan. 'Play this to your dad.' She dug Sadie's old batteries from her pocket. 'But use these.'

'Why?'

'Wee Sadie's duck wasn't flapping its wings – well it couldn't, because its batteries were wearing down, and – '

'Sadie's duck – you're losing me, Val.'

'Don't you see – the batteries were a bit flat – but not absolutely flat. So maybe – just maybe – they'll make the tape play at the right speed.'

Alan's finger was poised above the 'Play' button.

'No don't!' squealed Valentine. 'Not till your dad's listening. There's maybe only enough energy for one try. He's got to hear Bloodshot speaking.'

'Okay. But Dad thinks you're getting a bit carried away.' Alan got up.

'He does?' Valentine grabbed his arm. 'Well he'd better believe it. Bloodshot's back in the village.'

'How do you know?'

'Here's his van. And there he is.'

Bloodshot was clambering out, scratching at his armpit, his face red as an overcooked frankfurter. He lumbered into the shop belching loudly, and demanding 'twen'y mawlbra, an' a packit of indigestion tablits, quick-smart.'

Valentine pulled Alan behind the fish lorry. 'I've got to go. Phone me after you've played the tape to your dad.'

❧ • ❧

Heading homeward along the beach, Valentine saw the ferry-boat which delivered smolts. It was steaming away from the fish farm. Good.

But her mother was being angry down the phone again. 'What do you mean it wasn't your fault? Three of our nets ripped apart by your propellers, 45,000 salmon off to Greenland? It wasn't exactly the hand of God, was it?'

Valentine put the kettle on. A mug of tea would help calm her mother down.

Mrs Kerr slapped the phone down. She turned on Valentine. 'So, while they're pumping the new smolts into one cage, their stupid propellers are shredding the cages behind them – cages full of mature salmon we're on the point of selling. And they say it's just an accident?' She sat down at the table, her head in her hands and burst into tears.

Valentine dunked the teabag till the liquid looked about the right colour and added a splash of milk. She set the mug down in front of her mother, and gave her shoulder a squeeze.

Her mother sniffed. 'Tissue please?'

Valentine handed her one.

'Thanks. Sorry. It's just – they're so smug. I don't know how I'm going to tell Dad. It was – all over in a flash. All our savings have gone on this venture. I don't know what we'll do, now. A big escape like this – it's the last thing we needed.'

97

Valentine unwrapped the remains of her lunch. 'Eat this,' she said. 'Chocolate always helps.' She felt really sorry for her mother.

'Val, there are times when I wish I was teaching again. It was all so simple.'

While her mother sipped tea, Valentine's thoughts drifted to the newly freed salmon. Where would they go – straight for the open sea and the Atlantic feeding grounds, or up the river Mellish?

She remembered the killing weeks from February through till April when the mature fish were being harvested in their hundreds from the cages, brought in daily to be slaughtered, bled, packed into tubs of ice and sent off to a chain of supermarkets in the south. She knew that it was no different to harvesting a field of corn, or sending your fattened beef-cattle off to be turned into mince and burgers. She knew that the family's livelihood now depended on the commercial marketing of their fish. But part of her rejoiced in the feeling that some of these beautiful fish would now be free to roam the ocean.

Mum was calmer now. 'I suppose any job involving live creatures is bound to be fraught with difficulties. And I'm glad we decided to live here. I want to make a go of it. Today has just been – a bit much.'

Valentine gazed out of the window at the cattle on a nearby hill. 'It really is like land-farming.'

'It sounds so simple. But there's always something going wrong. The non-stop work. First thing in the morning, feed the fish. Maintenance all day; overhauling and cleaning the nets and cages, sorting the ropes. All the worry whenever the wind gets up, in case it's another storm. And salmon are so sensitive, so prone to stress with the slightest thing, even fluctuations in the water-temperature. They go off their food and get run-down. All the workers to pay each week; fish husbandrymen, maintenance men.' Her mother got up wearily. 'Thanks, dear, the tea was lovely. And your choccie bar.'

'Watch out *you* don't get over-stressed,' said Valentine. 'At least you've no problem with poaching – it's not like the river.'

Her mother stopped washing the mug and looked at her for a second. Then she went on, 'We do too. We only avoided it last month because Lachy the post knows everything that's going on.'

'Oh?'

'Yes. And I caught these "yachty" types dipping one of the cages.'

'Why? Yacht owners are loaded.'

'Who knows? For a lark? They don't stop to think the salmon are our living. Oh, Val, that reminds me – I'm supposed to be baking for tomorrow night. That wee theatre company's coming to the village hall again, and there's a dance afterwards.'

'Do it later.'

'No. I have to go to this meeting in the village.'

'I'll defrost the stuff we made last Sunday.'

'Good idea, Val. Now – I'll throw something together for supper, and you – you have a room to tidy?' Mrs Kerr hugged her daughter. 'Thanks for listening. I don't know what I'd do without you.'

Much later, Valentine telephoned Alan. 'Why didn't you call me?'

Alan's voice was sleepy. 'You woke me up. There was nothing to tell.'

Valentine's heart sank, 'The tape didn't work?'

'No. Dad and Mum went out before I'd a chance to play

it. Gran's here for the weekend and she sent me to bed.'

'Try again in the morning?'

'Maybe.' Alan didn't sound very convinced.

'Do it. Please.' Valentine put the phone down. She wasn't going to sleep much tonight.

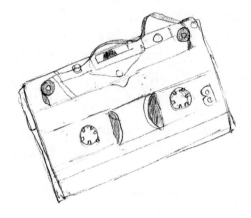

Friday

The air felt still and thick as Valentine walked to school. Purply grey clouds glowered over the sea, which gleamed darkly below them like a sheet of metal.

Alan, at the school gate, looked unhappy. 'Mum took the recorder off me. She hadn't time to listen.'

'What, with my tape in it?'

'Sorry, Val.' He shrugged. 'She needed it.'

'Oh no!' wailed Valentine. 'What if she records something over Bloodshot's voice?'

Alan looked shame-faced. 'I did say – '

'Alan, you're useless,' she flung away from him.

He ran after her 'Val wait. There's more – '

At that moment Mrs McCrindle appeared. 'Hurry along you two.'

Alan whispered, 'See you at lunchtime, *please* Val.'

'Maybe,' said Valentine.

The hours dragged by. The Munros were off school again. She been hoping to sort everything out with Coll, now she could trust him again. She wasn't sure if he'd want to be her friend any more. After all, she'd called him a dirty poacher.

Framed in the classroom window, the tide turned and the grey sea crept up the beach, merging with the river. It would be bringing the young salmon, the grilse which had been swimming homewards for weeks. She imagined them nosing innocently along the shore, seeking the taste of the river they'd left so long ago, happily recognising the Mellish, only to swim upstream to their doom tonight.

She couldn't concentrate on schoolwork for wondering, would Bloodshot use the spoof poison tin she'd planted in the poachers' bag? If so, the river might be safe. But what if he used Fanshawe's real poison?

At midday she waited for Alan. By now, the sea was leaden and the clouds so dark that the diving gulls looked like streaks of chalk on a blackboard.

Alan interrupted her thoughts. 'I had an idea, after you phoned me last night. So I just – went ahead and did it.'

'Did what?'

When he'd finished explaining, Valentine was deeply impressed. 'Brilliant,' she breathed.

'Dad would kill me if he knew – but, if it works – ' Alan threw a stone into the sea. 'Val, there's something else.'

'What?'

'Coll's old man's making him help, tonight.'

'Oh no!' Valentine was disgusted. 'What's his problem?'

'There's no way he can get out of it,' said Alan. 'That's why he stayed off school. He couldn't face you.'

'What a wooss!'

Alan stared at her. 'No. Coll thinks it's awful, what they're planning. But he has to do what his dad says.'

Valentine was furious. 'Oh no he doesn't! Hasn't he got a mind of his own? Why couldn't he – phone the police?'

'What, and turn his old man in?'

'Yes, if it's right. I'd do it. I'd do – anything, to save the river.' Valentine's voice tailed away as she remembered her own reluctance to tell. 'Well, almost anything.'

A rumble of distant thunder rolled round the bay.

Alan said, 'Calm down, Val. Whatever Coll's made to do, he's going to get a good look at the poachers. Which could be useful when they're caught.'

'*If* they're caught, it'll be too late to save the river,' she said. But, privately, Valentine was surprised how worried she was about Coll. Wouldn't he be in real danger, with a ruthless bunch like Bloodshot and his gang?

A tongue of silver lightning flickered along the horizon.

Suddenly she decided. There was no doubt, now, what she had to do after school.

It was time to stop worrying about her own freedom. Somehow, she must hand over the full story to an adult – and soon.

When she got home, a blue car was parked in the driveway. Dad was home! Forgetting everything else, Valentine rushed inside and threw herself into her father's arms. He smelled of wood-smoke and tweed.

'Hey there, Val, you nearly knocked me over. How's things?' He hugged her.

'Oh Dad, it's great you're back.'

'It's good to be home. I learned a lot at the conference, met some good people, but oh – these academics never know when to stop. I've got organic fish food coming out of my ears.'

She laughed.

'Val, do you know where Mum might have put the matches? I've been trying to light this stove.' Crumpled paper, sticks and logs littered the floor.

Valentine handed him the matches from their normal place on the shelf. 'Mum's feeling awful about losing all these fish while you were away.'

'I know,' he said. 'It's a bit of a shambles. I've been trying to find out about our insurance.' He struck a match and lit the paper. Flames licked up and the room began to smell warm and woody.

'It wasn't her fault,' said Valentine.

'Of course not. I'm taking her to the play tonight, to take her mind off it. Are you coming?' He lit the stove and the paper flamed up, droplets of rain spitting and sparking in the chimney.

'No thanks. I've to go up to Alan's – Oh, hi Mum.'

Her mother came in, dripping wet, her face white and strained. They had tea together in the kitchen, comfortably. Afterwards, Mum looked more cheerful. She said, 'Alan's Gran, brave woman, is putting on a video for any of you kids who don't want to go to the play. And everyone's welcome at the dance afterwards, as usual. She'll drive you down to the hall.'

Outside, the thunder rumbled. Mention of Alan brought back all Valentine's earlier anxiety. 'Mum, Dad, there's something I've *got* to tell you.'

'Make it snappy then. It's six-thirty already. We're late.' Her mother swept a lipstick over her mouth somewhat inaccurately with one hand and picked up the car keys with the other.

Her father drifted through the kitchen. 'What's up, Val?'

She only had time to tell the barest details before her mother interrupted, sternly. 'This really is none of your business, Val. Poaching's a regular summer problem here. Gavin McCrindle knows about these people, and he's perfectly capable of dealing with them – specially now he's got that nice Fanshawe girl working with him. And the poacher-watch scheme starts this weekend.'

'*Nice* Fanshawe – ?'

Her father said, 'Don't worry. We'll mention it to Gavin. Right – let's go. Fetch your things. We'll drop you off at Alan's road end. Okay?' He strode out to the car.

Her mother followed, calling, 'Switch on the answering machine will you, Val?'

Valentine sprayed her head with midge-repellent. Beside the answering machine was Dad's mobile phone. On impulse, she pocketed it.

At the road end, her mother said, 'It looks like it's going to bucket with rain. She dragged her old wax coat from under the seat. 'You'd better take this, Val. Straight to Alan's – and no trespassing on the river tonight. It's out of bounds to us all now.'

'Thanks to the Sheikh,' said Valentine with heavy sarcasm, carefully promising nothing. As casually as she could, she asked, 'When's the play due to finish?' If this was to be her last night of freedom, she needed to know how long she'd got.

❧ • ❧

The first drops of rain began to fall as Valentine reached the fork in the road to Alan's house. She dialled his number on the mobile. 'Alan, can you come out? I'm going up to the Salmon Leap to see what happens.'

She heard him shout to his Gran then there was a pause. Little clouds of midges made grey smudges among the raindrops. Alan's voice came on the phone. There was a problem. His mother had been hurt. They were just deciding whether to take her to the surgery or to hospital. If he could get out, he'd meet her at the Salmon Leap later.

Uneasily, Valentine pulled on her mother's jacket. What could have happened to Mrs McCrindle?

She set off up the grassy track towards the old bridge. The verges were shoulder-high with dying bluebells so that she was walking through wafts of perfume, till her nose detected diesel smoke.

The bridge arched high over the river, all knobbly stones and weeds. She couldn't see over it. She stopped, listening. Thunder was rumbling lazily round the hills and the air was warm and humid. Through the rattling of the river came the sound of an engine.

Hoping Mum's jacket would camouflage her, she crouched low and began to run over the bridge.

From the top of its humpy back she could see where the track ended in a tangle of undergrowth. Away beyond lay the forbidden parklands of Ardmellish Estate. A single sunbeam shone through the clouds, its glow gilding the lawns and the stately trees and the house itself till it looked like a golden city. Was that a light in one of the ground floor rooms? No, it couldn't be, for no-one now lived there, and Mrs Munro would have finished work hours ago.

Near the bridge end sat two vans, one dirty white, the other, rusty yellow. Valentine's heart pounded. Bloodshot and Fanshawe! Both vehicles looked empty, though the white van's engine was running. She watched, poised to run. Nothing moved. If the poachers had started already, she'd stop them getting away.

She crawled to the side of Bloodshot's van. With her ballpoint pen, she went round the tyres, pushing in the valve pins till the air hissed out. Getting bolder, she tried the doors. Both were locked. A black balaclava helmet lay squashed in the mud.

She slithered to Fanshawe's van and flattened the rear tyres. The back window was obscured by black bags. She crept round the side, reaching up to try the passenger door. No handle. She flattened the front tyre. She made for the driver's door. To her surprise it was slightly open. She was sure –

A hand grabbed her wrist!

She pulled away, but the hand gripped like a vice. 'Val!'

'Coll!'

'What are you doin' here?' Coll's head appeared, his eyes goggling. 'I had their Walkman on. I didnae hear you.' He yanked the earphones off.

Valentine shook with shock.

'It's okay,' Coll said. 'They're away for chips.'

'Chips?' she said, vaguely.

'I'm the look out,' he winked.

Valentine tried to pull her wits together. 'Coll, undo the bonnet catch?'

The bonnet popped up. 'No' a very good watchman, eh?' Coll smiled.

Valentine yanked out all the wires she could see. A cup-shaped object came away in her hands.

'The distributor,' said Coll, stretching.

She stuffed it into her pocket. 'And – Bloodshot's van?'

'They took the keys.' Coll looked at her. Then he said quietly 'Don't worry, I'll see tae it. When they're – busy.' He stood up, looking down-river. He whispered urgently 'Val, they're comin'. Run for it!'

Bent low, Valentine raced back across the bridge. She fell into the bluebells. Only just in time. The poachers passed within yards of her. She could smell their fish suppers! Fanshawe's cackling laugh rattled her nerves.

As soon as the poachers reached the vans, Valentine headed up the glen. She came out on an escarpment from which she could see the whole of Glenmellish, right down to the loch. It had grown so dark, the street lights had come on down in the village. Someone must have lit a bonfire in the quarry. A thin plume of smoke drifted from it, and the smell of burning rubbish drifted along the hillside.

A snap of lightning sent her running into the trees above the Salmon Leap.

In the shadowy wood the river poured along, a mysterious flow, gleaming black between its banks. Valentine kept away from the path, moving between the tree-trunks, the leaf-litter muffling her footfalls. When she reached the long pool that topped the waterfall, she paused, listening again. It was the time of evening when birds go quiet, and animals wait for darkness before venturing out. The only sound was the soft splashing of the waterfall below.

Crump! The thunder was much nearer now. Thud! Something landed at her feet. Her heart almost stopped. What was it? Light footsteps skittered away. She bent and picked up something heavy, wrapped in paper.

Breathless with fright, she ran slipping and sliding down the slope by the waterfall till she reached the beech tree. She swung herself onto the lowest branch. She wouldn't feel safe till she was high in its leafy canopy.

Only when she was astride her branch did she remember you weren't supposed to go near trees in a thunderstorm, in case they were struck by lightning.

She unwrapped the package. It was a stone, covered with a FORM newsletter. She could just make out the rough writing on the back.

'Disconnexted van battery's. Now they've no engine, and no refriggerotor. Good??? Sadie's bringing this. She shoodny have came out. I've tellt her AWA HAME ye wee bisiom. Love, Coll.'

❧ • ❧

The storm was almost overhead by the time Alan appeared. Lightning flashed again as he scrambled up to the branch below Valentine's. He shone a torch up at her.

'Switch that thing off, it's blinding me,' she whispered, glad she was no longer alone.

'Sorry I'm late,' he panted.

'Is your mum okay?'

'Her face is in an awful mess.'

'What happened?'

'Dad thinks they've broken some of her ribs. The doctor's seeing her now. She's fed up.'

'Oh, poor Mrs McCrindle. Who –?'

'They had balaclavas on, but she's sure one was a woman. Mum was taking her trout rod over the bridge pool after school. These thugs showed up. They handed her a note with her car number on it, "Is this yours, Mrs?" She was to get off the river, or they'd do her car in. She said to get lost, she'd a permit – next thing they were beating her up.'

'That's disgusting,' said Valentine.

Alan's voice shook, 'She managed to get herself home. But if I ever get a chance – '

'Calm down.' But Valentine couldn't help thinking – no bailiff on the river, tonight of all nights. 'Look.' She showed him Coll's note. This would take his mind off. 'Coll's bust Bloodshot's van, so the poachers can't get away.' She giggled.

Alan grunted, 'I told you he was with us.'

'I know,' said Valentine. 'It's great.'

Alan said, 'Val, we'd better go home. I said to Gran I'd bring you.'

'Oh no. I'm staying. Specially if your dad can't come out on duty.' Valentine shivered a little.

'I think it's too late, anyway,' Alan's voice was quiet. 'Here they come.'

Darkness had fallen like a cloak The rain seemed colder. Someone was lumbering along, lugging a sack. Alan shone his torch down, lighting up red hair in its beam. 'Coll!'

Coll dropped the bag. 'Who –? Oh it's yous. Put that thing out. They'll see us.'

'Where are they?' Alan switched it off.

'Right behind me,' said Coll. 'Did wee Sadie –?'

'Yes, she's away,' said Valentine. 'It's – brilliant, what you did.'

Coll laughed softly. 'It's a right mess. Half 'o the fellas got lost. Fanshawe's caravan's on fire and she's ragin'. Watch out for her, by the way. She's got night-sights. She'll can see you as clear as daylight.'

Alan whispered, 'Who else?'

'Some fellas I don't know. I wis sent down tae watch who went intae the hall for the play. Auld Nick and the bailiff didnae go. My Mum was cryin' at the door. Daddy promised tae take her, and he wisnae there. I don't know where he is.' He looked around nervously. 'I've tae get the rest o' the stuff.' He disappeared down the path.

The moon came out, full and round, making the waterfall gleam silver against the black rocks, and turning the trees the colour of dead bones.

Valentine heard the sound of oilskin trousers brushing together, then low voices, then the riverbank filled with the dark shapes of people.

Far away, an unearthly howl split the night.

Bloodshot sniffed noisily, then spat. 'That dawg sounds like the blood'ound wot was 'ere last weekend.' He leaned his back against the tree, just as he had last Saturday, and lit up a cigarette. 'Right you boys, no time to wiste.' His high voice sent fear shimmering through Valentine's veins.

A motorbike came spluttering up the path. Mr Munro's

Yamaha. It stopped with a loud backfire.

'Would ya like to mike a bit more noise?' Bloodshot muttered through a stream of smoke. 'The lite Mr Munro. Is it all clear dahn at the road end then?'

'Aye,' said Mr Munro. 'They're all in at the play.' Lightning flashed.

Thunder crashed. Bloodshot snorted, 'Wot is it – Lays Mis'rables eh? Time to get started folks. Where's the stuff?' He dug about in one of the black bags.

Fanshawe opened another. She held up a tin and kissed it dramatically. 'Heah you are.'

Bloodshot produced an identical tin from his bag. 'No, this is it. Ow, give me strength. Urry along there Fanshawe. Bash some 'oles in it. We 'aven't got all night.'

'Wot with?' she asked.

'Wotever you like darlin'. 'Ow about your luvly fingerniles?' Bloodshot's belly shook with laughter.

One of his gang produced a screwdriver and Fanshawe began punching holes in her tin. Little puffs of white powder came out.

'Munro, you know the water,' said Bloodshot. 'Ware's the best plice to put the stuff?'

Davy switched on the Yamaha's headlamp, using it as a pointer. 'As near tae the waterfall as possible' he said slowly. 'Tae catch the flow.'

Coll stood behind his father, head down.

Fanshawe picked up the pockmarked tin.

Bloodshot tried to grab it. 'Give it to Munro, 'e knows wot e's doin' 'ere.'

Fanshawe hung on to her tin. 'I can throw it just as well as him.' She kicked Bloodshot's legs. 'Get awff.'

'Bloody women's libber. I said give it to 'im, so you'll give it to 'im. You're supposed to be lookin' after the van and keepin' an eye out for – er intruders.'

'I'm not leaving all the fish to you scumbags.' Fanshawe swore at him.

Next thing, they were fighting, in the dimming light from the Yamaha, Bloodshot cursing, Fanshawe squawking. Bloodshot got hold of her hair and pulled. She scratched long red gouges out of his face.

The other men began to laugh, which only seemed to enrage the combatants more.

Coll moved silently away, the moonlight shadowing him.

Fanshawe and Bloodshot staggered nearer and nearer the water's edge.

The Yamaha's light went out. There came a soft, sliding thump, followed by two splashes, a squeal and a glugging shout. Bloodshot and Fanshawe had disappeared into the pool.

The water thrashed and boiled, then Bloodshot surfaced, yelling, 'C'mon boys, 'elp me, I can't swim!'

The stick-like shape of Fanshawe struggled beside him, gurgling, 'I say, wait for me. Help, I'm being poisoned!'

The men reached out with long gaffs. With difficulty they hooked the two struggling bundles of clothing. They dragged them to the bank, where they lay gasping like a pair of beached fish.

Mr Munro's voice was flat as he said, 'That's done it. They've left the poison in the water, right enough. It'll start tae work now.' He turned round to look behind him. 'Coll? Coll, where are you, son?' Slowly he laid the bike on its side.

The centre of the pool went quiet for a moment. Somewhere in the wood a vixen barked to her mate. After a moment came his reply. The pool's surface reflected whorls of moonlight. Suddenly one of them erupted. A circle

of bubbles popped and fizzed.

'That's it, boys,' Bloodshot's voice was gleeful. 'Wite for it. Oho, we're gonna be rich!' He got to his feet, water cascading out of his clothes. 'Viva España, 'ere we come!'

At that moment everything went pitch dark. From overhead, the whirring of an engine turned to a roar.

An explosion of brilliant light burst from the sky. The whole scene was illuminated, the black shapes of the men backing away into the trees, shielding their eyes from the dazzle of the helicopter's lamp.

A star-shape of searchlight beams flared from between the trees, criss-crossing the clearing, chasing the escapees out of the wood, back to the river. Advancing towards them, was a small bandy-legged man, Auld Nick, with his enormous dog on a leash. He unclipped it. 'Go for them Bounder. And remember, son, I didn't tell you to be careful.'

Saturday

Valentine woke slowly. Music played softly downstairs. She opened her eyes. A sunbeam shone between the curtains. She squinted at the clock. Midday. Oh no! She sat up. Then she slithered slowly and deliciously under her warm duvet again. It was Saturday. There was no school.

Her mother's head appeared round the door. 'Thought you might be hungry.' The warm smell of toast wafted from the tray she laid beside Valentine's bed. She sat down. 'We slept in too. What a night – all of us dancing the eightsome reel with our muddy boots on!'

Valentine laughed.

'Take your toast, dear. And did you see Maddy Munro? She was just like wee Sadie.'

Valentine sat up. 'She got Davy to dance.'

'Which I've never seen before. He was – quite merry.'

Valentine sipped orange juice.

Her mother went on, 'Coll's just off the phone. I told him

117

you weren't awake yet. They're all very relieved. Apparently Mr Hassan isn't going to press charges against Davy. "Insufficient evidence".'

Valentine bit into the toast. 'And the river's been saved.'

'Davy Munro's never been in trouble before.'

Valentine wiped butter off her chin. 'He wanted to get even with the Sheikh, for making him redundant.'

Her mother frowned. 'Understandable. But he shouldn't have – '

'No.' Valentine agreed. 'Baking-powder was better.'

Her mother smiled. 'So the scones weren't a waste of time, last Sunday?'

Valentine giggled. 'Like you said – baking-powder goes fizzy in water just like rabbit-gas. I thought Bloodshot would throw it in the river, and it would *look* like what he was expecting – but the fish wouldn't die, and he'd go away and never come back.'

Her mother said, 'Very clever, but *very* dangerous. Why on earth didn't you say anything?'

'I did. I told Stuart Laurie, I sent the tape to Mr McCrindle, and last of all I *tried* to tell you yesterday, but – well – everything seemed to go wrong.'

'Why me last?'

'Because – oh Mum, I thought – if you knew about Bloodshot's gang – you'd be too scared to let me out any more.'

'Too scared?' her mother fulminated, 'a bit more careful, perhaps. But freedom is what we've come here for. There's no way I'm about to let disgusting people like "Bloodshot" and Fenella Fanshawe spoil our lives.' Mum could sound quite magnificent. 'Gavin McCrindle's delighted they've been caught. It turns out most of the gang are wanted for poaching all over Scotland.'

Valentine sipped orange juice. 'What happens now?'

'At this moment the poachers will be taking a last look at the scenery, on their way down Loch Lomond. Stuart's colleagues are driving them to – er – more secure accommodation in town. Gavin reckons it'll be a long time before any of them sees the light of day on a river again.'

'Whew,' said Valentine.

Her mother stood up. 'Yes, *but*, young lady, if everyone took the law into their own hands, there'd be chaos.'

'And if you don't follow your – your conscience,' retorted Valentine, 'You might as well be a computer. I thought Coll was just going to do everything his father told him to, like – like a sheep. But I was wrong about him,' she said more thoughtfully. 'He does care about the river.'

'Better a live sheep than a dead hero,' her mother's face was serious. 'I'm very glad you're safe. Unlike poor Mary McCrindle.'

Valentine laughed. 'Wasn't she amazing at the dance? Hopping about on her crutches.' Then she saw her mother's expression. 'Oh, Mum, I'm *really* sorry I made you worry.'

'Yes, well the scars on Mary McCrindle's face will remind me, for a long time, what might have happened to you if Bloodshot and his gang had caught you.'

Valentine felt as deflated as Bloodshot's tyres. 'Kids can't really do anything useful, on their own.'

Mrs Kerr shook her head, 'Not true. If it hadn't been for you alerting me last weekend – '

'You mean – you believed me *then*?' Valentine squeaked.

'You'd obviously seen poachers. That's why we held a meeting on Thursday night. Auld Nick was actually watching the river last Saturday. He'd been told that poachers were likely to be coming into the area soon, but didn't know who they were. He thought Bounder had given him away, by barking. When you identified "Bloodshot" to Stuart, he passed his description, and the registration number of his stolen van, to all the police in the district. After that Bloodshot couldn't make a move without it being known.'

'I see.' Valentine's voice was small.

Her mother said, 'Cheer up. Your twelfth birthday's next week. Wasn't it a twelve-year-old girl who dreamed up the first International Children's Conference on the Environment in the nineties? *And* made it happen?'

'Yes, but, she didn't have to put her friends in danger, did she? Mum, why didn't you tell me you knew?'

'Because we wanted you kids safely out of the way. We thought, if you knew, you'd try to watch – dangerous – and likely mess up our plans.'

'So, why wasn't Bloodshot caught before?'

'Gavin McCrindle and the police wanted to catch the whole gang red-handed. Put the whole lot of them away, not just one man.'

'Right,' breathed Valentine. 'And we nearly gave the game away.'

'Best to leave stuff like that to the professionals, eh, Val?'

Valentine said, 'Maybe I'll stick to writing the newsletter for FORM. There'll be quite a bit to report this week.' She laughed, remembering, 'I've still got Bloodshot's beer can in my school bag. I thought there might be fingerprints.'

'Sherlock Holmes,' her mother picked up the tray. 'It's a lovely day – the thunderstorm did clear the air beautifully. We've invited everyone here for a celebration barbecue tonight. Will you give me a hand?'

All afternoon Valentine helped her parents prepare for the party. She defrosted food, decorated puddings, stuck sticks into sausages, collected driftwood from the shore and set out tables on the rough grass between the house and the sea.

When everything was ready, they stopped for a break. Valentine decided to test her parents' theory about freedom. 'Can I – go out for a while?' She needed peace and quiet to sort out her thoughts before seeing everyone again. Before meeting Coll.

Her mother smiled at her father. 'Don't see why not. You're old enough to look after yourself now, aren't you?'

❧ • ❧

In the late afternoon sunshine, Valentine ran up the riverside road. Someone had cut down the 'PRIVATE' notice, which lay in the long grass. She ran on up the riverside all the way to the Salmon Leap.

This time, she didn't bother climbing her tree. She felt quite safe sitting on the warm ground, leaning against its trunk, enjoying the feelings of peace and privacy. Bees buzzed among the green dangling flowers of a nearby maple, whose honey-scent perfumed the air. Dozens of aerobatic swallows swooped and soared over the sparkling river, hunting midges and mayfly.

The waterfall must have been there for thousands of years, wearing its way down through the rocky cleft. The sun was bouncing rainbows off the spray.

How different from last night. The arrival of the Sheikh, Mr Hassan, in his helicopter, Gavin McCrindle's voice booming from behind a torch beam: 'Deus ex machina – God comes in the machine! See to that Fanshawe, Bracken. Go on, girl.' Auld Nick: 'After him, Bounder.' The delighted woofing of the big dog as he grabbed Bloodshot, dripping saliva from his loose jowls. Both dogs snarling, hanging on to the terrified poachers.

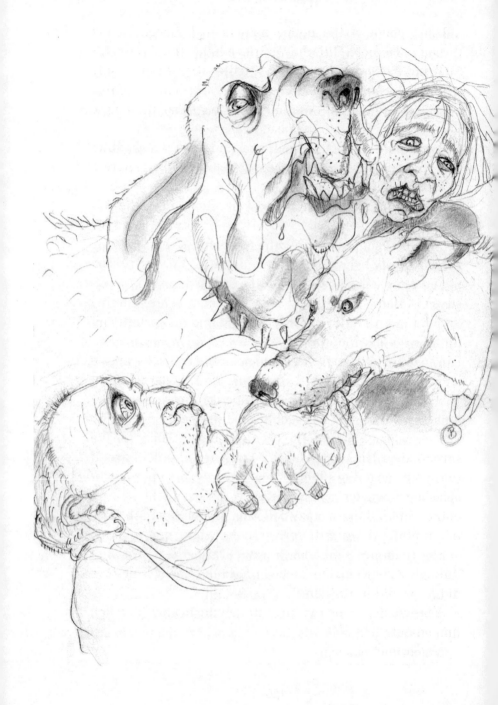

Later, some of the police helpers had dragged a net through the pool, till they retrieved the tin. When Mr McCrindle opened it, at her insistence, they'd found only a few grains of undissolved baking-powder. The tin of real poison they found in another black bag, just what they needed to incriminate the poachers.

Afterwards, Auld Nick had come out from the shadows and clamped a hand on Mr Munro's shoulder. 'I'll have a word with you, Davy.'

She would never forget the look of relief on Mr Munro's face, though he only said, 'There's no fish killed, man.'

She dreamed, watching the peaceful river, bringing herself slowly back to this lovely day.

Suddenly, a fish jumped, sending ripples across the pool's silken surface. It fell back, then appeared again, surging into the air. In a flurry of spray the wild salmon hurled itself up towards the waterfall. The torrent flung it down again like an old sock. It leapt yet again, its shining muscles urging it upward. Valentine could practically feel its determination as its body flexed and arched, desperate to reach the top, four times, five, six, and each time the waterfall won.

There came a pause. The river quietened. Then, for the seventh time, the salmon leaped. Streaking high out beyond the spray, gleaming silver, it flew towards the top. There it splashed down, wriggling frantically, poised on the very lip of the waterfall like a crazy ballerina, till, with a flash of its tail, it plunged onward, upriver, out of sight, and safe.

The river was safe, too. A wave of sheer elation swept through Valentine. She danced round the tree yelling, 'We did it, we did it. Brilliant!'

A brown dog came rustling through the bushes. Bracken limped out.

'Valentine?'

'Coll!'

He gave his slow smile. 'Revisitin' the scene of the crime?'

Valentine was watching the river again. 'Did you see that salmon?'

'Aye, I saw it.'

'D'you think wishing can make something happen? I mean, like I was *willing* it to reach the top of the waterfall.'

'I think the fish was wishin' quite hard itself. Its instinct's tellin' it tae go upstream and find a mate.'

Valentine laughed. 'Trust you to be sensible. But it's – amazing, that a fish can be so – so brave-hearted.'

Coll grinned. 'I like that.'

'What?'

'You sayin' "trust me". Will you be trustin' me from now on? That's what me and Bracken need tae know, don't we girl?' He stroked the dog's shining head and she looked adoringly up at him, wagging her tail.

Valentine felt herself blushing. 'I'm sorry Coll – for not believing you. You were brilliant last night. Are you coming to the barbie?'

'Am I invited?' His face had gone back to its normal cheeky grin.

They walked down the river path together, going over and over the events of last night.

Valentine ran round the corner of the house, feeling happy. She smelt wood smoke and charcoal and delicious food. Dad, his face red with heat, and an old fishmonger's apron round his middle, was laying potatoes in rows over the fire.

Mum came across the grass with two large jugs of Sangria. 'We're going to barbecue a couple of salmon. A sort of sacrifice to the Gods or something, in the hope they'll smile on the fish farm from now on. It looks as if the insurance company is going to pay up for the damage, after all.'

The party was a great success. Most of the people from the village came; Auld Nick brought Bounder, who spent the entire time looking so sorrowfully at the burgers dripping into the flames that everyone gave him titbits. The McCrindles came, although Mrs McCrindle's face was hidden by a scarf and dark glasses. Lia stayed close to her side, looking anxiously up at her. The Munros came too, Davy sporting a new sweater and wee Sadie clutching a new doll.

Everyone had brought food and drink to add to the barbecue, and the trestle table groaned with goodies; salads glistening with wonderful dressings, bowlfuls of potatoes roasted, fried, chopped with chives. There were puddings of all kinds from jellies and trifles to apple crumble and chocolate mousse. Bottles of wine nudged sides with huge containers of Irn Bru, lemonade and orange juice.

Just as Lachy the postman struck up the first notes on his accordion to begin the dancing, a bright blue helicopter swished down from the sky, its slipstream blowing smoke from the barbecue all over the crowd. It alighted on the grass like a big dragonfly. The door opened and a tall dark-skinned man in an immaculate white suit leapt down.

'The Sheikh,' said Davy Munro. 'Mr Hassan.'

Mr Hassan held up his arms and lifted down a tall pale boy with a mop of black hair. The boy leaned against him while someone unfolded a wheelchair. Slowly they came across the lawn, and everyone crowded round.

Mr Hassan spoke with a slightly American accent, introducing himself. Then he said, 'I have brought my son, Hanuf, from the hospital in town.'

Hanuf said, 'Which of you sent me the e-mail?'

Alan was pushed to the front of the crowd, his father

staring at him in disbelief.

'I'd like to thank you, young man,' Mr Hassan shook Alan's hand. 'Hanuf looks after my e-mails when I'm travelling, only relaying important messages, like yours.'

Hanuf said, 'I can travel the world too, on the Internet.'

Soon he and Alan were deep in conversation.

Mr Hassan said, 'The doctors are pleased with his progress. He's well enough to stay for the weekend.' He looked around. 'Ah, it's too long since I came to take a look at my place here. I had forgotten how beautiful it is.'

To begin with, all the talk was about last night. Then the adults had an informal meeting, after which Gavin McCrindle made some announcements. 'Ardmellish Estate – has been suffering – a degree of under-manning. Mr Hassan has agreed that more people should be employed in future. Perhaps, Mr Nicholas, you would like to explain?'

Auld Nick got up, a large whisky in his glass, his cheeks an unusually merry scarlet. He climbed onto a rock. 'Aye, Gavin has it right. We're to appoint a full-time ghillie again, to look after the rivers. And Davy Munro, if you're willing, the job is yours. On the recommendation of the bailiff hisself. Permanent.'

Mr Munro gave a gasp of surprise. Coll and Sadie whooped, and hugged their mother. Someone muttered 'Set a thief to catch a thief,' and everyone cheered.

Auld Nick went on 'We've agreed to take on the fish farm as part of the estate. The Kerrs will continue to run it, but we'll finance it, so we can – improve the facilities. And we're to build a hatchery upriver, to encourage the stock in the river, and to give winter employment. There'll be a smoking business set up, so we can process our own produce and sell it right here from the village. So we'll be looking for youngsters to train up.'

The sun reddened, and slid towards the horizon of Loch Mellish as everyone danced to Lachy's accordion. The dogs pranced about happily among the throng. Wee Sadie plied Hanuf with sweets, and skipped round him, singing and twinkling her eyes at him till he laughed as loudly as the rest.

Much later the moon rose over the loch. Valentine sat on a rock, little wavelets frisking at her feet, feeling full of happiness, thinking how great it was to have a friend like Coll, someone she could really trust. She said, 'This has been the best day.'

'Aye, no' bad,' said Coll.

'The fish and the river are okay.'

'They'll be okay till the next time you get up there wi' your rod.'

Valentine leaped off the rock and grabbed his hand. Together they ran along the moonlit beach, singing at the top of their voices, splashing in and out of the waves, sprinting through the phosphorescence like a couple of salmon on the spring run.